39 Castles: BOOK ONE
Greengrove Castle

39 Castles: BOOK ONE

GREENGROVE CASTLE

Matt Thorne

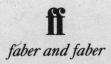

faber and faber

First published in 2004
by Faber and Faber Limited
3 Queen Square London WC1N 3AU

Typeset by Faber and Faber Limited
Printed in England by Mackays of Chatham plc, Chatham, Kent

A CIP record for this book
is available from the British Library
ISBN 0–571–21996–9

2 4 6 8 10 9 7 5 3 1

For Alexandra Heminsley and Lesley Shaw,
Eleanor's first friends.

CASTLE SEVEN

Peace through Friendship

Castle Seven: The Rules

1 Never belittle the group or any individual in it.

2 Never draw your sword unless absolutely necessary.

3 If flattered, watch out for an ulterior motive.

4 If insulted, bear it lightly and never lose your temper.

Castle Seven: The Members

Anderson: the strongest man in the group. He is in his early thirties with long black hair and a thick beard. He is calm and confident.

Alexandra: the female leader. She is in her mid-twenties with fine, honey-coloured hair and blue eyes. She is trustworthy and considerate.

Sarah: the great-great-granddaughter of the last princess before the fall of the kingdom. She is serene, reserved and full of secrets.

Katharine: she has black hair and isn't that keen on children. She is extraordinarily composed at all times.

Lucinda: she used to work in an Inn, and has only recently joined the Clearheart Castle. Kind to Eleanor and always sympathetic, but a young-seeming adult.

Zoran: the joker of the group. Always looking for a good night out, and not to be trusted with even the simplest tasks.

Robert: Zoran's sidekick. He is more careful than his friend, but is still liable to cause chaos. He has blond curly hair and is in his mid-twenties.

Castle Factfiles

Plans

Ground
Floor

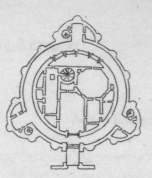

First
Floor

Second
Floor

GREENGROVE CASTLE

Facts and Figures

Community population: 12,000

Language spoken: English

Number of schools: 6

Size of army: 400 soldiers

Access to castle: limited to Basker, Basker's family
and his staff

Currency: Ballars

Castle library: large, but not available for access,
even to Basker's family

Plans

Ground Floor

First Floor

Second Floor

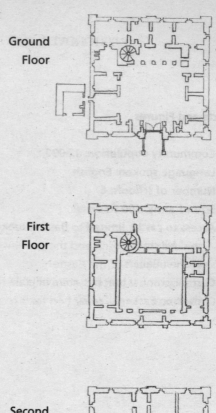

CLEARHEART CASTLE

Facts and Figures

Community population: 8,000
Language spoken: English
Number of schools: 4
Size of army: 200 soldiers
Access to castle: limited to the Castle Seven,
   the children chosen and the staff involved
   in the upkeep of the Castle
Currency: none; barter system in place
Castle library: small, reliant on texts copied

GREENGROVE CASTLE

This book takes place in a future that seems like the past.
After the fall of the kingdom, everyone in England has
divided themselves into thirty-nine communities, each
arranged around a different castle, apart from those who
have chosen to live in the wilderness . . .

CHAPTER ONE

On the eve of her twelfth birthday, a wonderful
thing happened to Eleanor Conway that changed
her life for ever.

It would be a while before Eleanor discovered
exactly why she had been chosen. When Anderson
arrived at her parents' door, they seemed scared,
especially when he produced a present for Eleanor.
At first she worried Anderson had come to ask her
parents to leave the Castle's grounds, and the present
was a way of softening the blow. But then she
overheard her own name being mentioned several
times. Eleanor couldn't remember doing anything
wrong, but everyone's behaviour was monitored
closely in the community and it was possible she'd
committed a small crime without realising it. As her
dread became unbearable, Anderson opened the door.

Eleanor immediately jumped back, more out of
surprise than alarm. Anderson didn't seem to notice,
asking where he should sit. Eleanor gestured nervously
to her small bed, which sagged heavily as he lowered
himself down. Anderson was only in his early thirties,

but he had long black hair and a thick beard and acted as if he was always ready to go into battle. Many of the younger children were scared of him, but Eleanor had an instinctive sense that he was a good man and would cause her no harm.

'Eleanor,' he asked, 'do you enjoy your classes?'

Adults often asked Eleanor this sort of question. Sometimes Eleanor pretended she didn't like her teachers, as that seemed to amuse them, but today she sensed Anderson wanted the truth, so she said, 'Yes, Anderson, I do.'

He smiled. 'What's your favourite lesson?'

'I like reading and writing. And music, although I'm not very good at it. The only instrument I can play properly is the recorder.'

'You can learn the others in time. Let me ask you a question, Eleanor. If you could be good at many things, or a master of one, which would you choose?'

Eleanor looked at Anderson. She felt slightly scared by the intensity behind his blue eyes as he stared at her. These weren't the casual questions an adult might ask while trying to make conversation with her at church or some social gathering. For the first time in her life, Eleanor felt as though someone valued her opinion. There was something behind these questions, and she realised that answering in the right way was extremely important. But what was the right way? Did Anderson want her to tell him the truth, or come up with an answer that matched his own belief? She had an uncanny sense that he could see right inside her

4

heart and realised that her only option was to be honest.

'If I could spend the rest of my life reading and writing stories, I would always be happy.'

Anderson thought for a moment, then gave a slow nod. Eleanor felt a sense of elation as she realised she had said the right thing. His next question was uttered in a more casual, offhand fashion, as if to let her know that she should continue to tell the truth. 'Can you ride, Eleanor?'

Eleanor looked down at the ground. 'No. I love horses, but my father had to sell his before I was born. My friends ride the wild horses down towards the river, but my parents won't let me go with them.'

'Your parents are sensible,' said Anderson, 'but it is a skill you must have. When you have a horse of your own, you will pick up the discipline quickly.'

'A horse of my own?' asked Eleanor.

'Yes.' He handed her the present he had brought. 'Don't open this until tomorrow.'

'OK.'

He stood up. 'Eleanor, have you ever met any of the Castle Seven?'

'No.'

'Do you know who they are?'

'No.'

'Your parents have never spoken of them?'

She shook her head.

'It doesn't matter,' he said. 'I suppose you know little of life inside the Castle.'

'My parents don't like me to go there too often.'

He nodded. 'I understand their concern. But your life is going to be different from now on. I'll come back to pick you up on Monday.'

Anderson left her bedroom. Eleanor waited until he had said goodbye to her parents, and then she went downstairs. Her father was sitting at a table, staring into the darkness. She went through to the kitchen, where her mother was cowering.

'What's wrong?' Eleanor asked.

'You didn't tell me you were doing so well at school.'

Eleanor felt embarrassed. She had long since stopped telling her mother about her classroom achievements as she always seemed worried whenever Eleanor did anything that brought her to the teacher's attention.

'What did he bring you?' her mother, April, asked.

'Anderson told me not to open it until tomorrow.'

'Yes, yes,' said April, 'quite right.'

That night, as on many nights, Eleanor had trouble getting to sleep. She could never normally sleep on the night before her birthday, or Christmas Eve, but now she had this new reason to feel excited. If it was up to Eleanor, she would read all night every night, but her mum and dad said it was bad for her eyes and they would allow her to read for only twenty minutes before they came in to extinguish her candle. She didn't know why they did this because she didn't sleep for ages, and it was far more interesting to read than to lie awake in the dark with nothing to do. Both her parents slept like logs from the moment their heads hit the pillow, so they had no understanding how boring being alone at night could be.

Eventually, however, Eleanor managed to drop off. That night her dreams were unusually exciting. She saw herself dancing with a tall, handsome boy. They were alone in a large banqueting hall. Candles in the far corners of the room were the only illumination, and no matter how hard she tried, Eleanor couldn't see the boy's face. Then, without warning, the dream changed to a much darker vision. Eleanor suddenly found herself locked in a dungeon. No one was ever allowed to see what happened in the dungeons, and Eleanor had had several nightmares about being trapped in one before. In this dream at first she only sensed she was in a dungeon, as she was surrounded by blackness and couldn't see anything at all. Gradually, her eyes became used to the dark and she began to crawl to what seemed like a tiny sliver of pale light in the far corner. As she crawled, she felt thick, mouldy straw against her knees and then her hand touched something hard and brittle. Before she could identify it, a skeleton suddenly sat up and grabbed her. She screamed, and, with her scream, woke up.

After her terrible nightmare, Eleanor didn't want to stay alone in her bed, but she told herself to be brave and tried to will herself back to sleep. Although she was generally very sensible, there were two things that terrified Eleanor, and these things often appeared in her dreams. The first were skeletons.

Eleanor knew that skeletons couldn't really come to life, but somehow when she went to sleep she always seemed to forget this. The second things were wolves. Eleanor was more afraid of wolves than anything else in the world. But after she had checked under the bed and locked her windows, she was satisfied that she wasn't in any danger tonight.

CHAPTER TWO

The following morning, Eleanor awoke as soon as it was light outside. She was too excited to stay asleep, and wanted to see what the day had in store. Rushing to the bottom of her bed, she found the present Anderson had given her and ripped the brightly coloured wrapping-paper from the small rectangular package. She could tell it was a book of some sort and was intrigued to discover what sort of story Anderson wanted her to read. But after she'd removed the wrapping-paper she realised, with a sinking heart, that Anderson had given her a dictionary. It wasn't that she didn't feel grateful, but she couldn't understand why he'd made a big deal out of such a boring present. The book was beautifully bound in burgundy leather, and each page had been carefully transcribed in elegant brown ink, but it wasn't what she'd been expecting.

Before the disappointment could spoil the excitement of her birthday morning, Eleanor's mother came through her bedroom door and said, 'Oh, Ellie, I'm glad you're awake. Mary's here and she's brought a present for you.'

9

Eleanor jumped up and followed her mother through to the front room. Mary was Eleanor's best friend. She was only a few days younger than Eleanor, and they had become friends on the day they'd met.

Mary was small, with an innocent smile, big blue eyes and bright red hair. She had a keen awareness of injustice, and if she ever witnessed any bullying in the playground, she'd always be the first to jump in and stop the fight, which would frequently get her into trouble. Eleanor's parents were extremely fond of Mary and happy to let her stay at their house, even on school nights.

Mary blushed as she handed Eleanor a present. 'It's not very exciting. But I hope you like it.'

Eleanor opened Mary's present. It was a small hand mirror, with a mother-of-pearl setting.

April looked over and said, 'Eleanor, why don't you tell Mary your news?'

Mary looked at Eleanor expectantly. As much as she loved her mother, Eleanor wished she hadn't brought this up yet.

'Oh,' she said, 'it's nothing important.'

April put her hands on Mary's shoulder and explained. 'Ellie's been asked to do something with people from the Castle. It means she won't be having classes with you for a while.'

'The Castle?' Mary asked, her eyes wide.

Eleanor couldn't help feeling a certain pride as she said, 'Anderson came to see me yesterday.'

'Anderson!' said Mary. 'I can't believe it. That's amazing.'

'I know,' Eleanor replied. 'I don't have any choice, Mary. I have to do what he asks.'

'So,' Mary said quickly, 'is Anderson your friend now?'

'I suppose so. He bought me a birthday present.'

'That's amazing,' Mary gushed. 'Can you talk to him at church tonight? Can you tell him I'm your friend?'

'I don't think you should be too informal,' said April nervously.

'It's fine,' Eleanor said decisively. 'I'm sure he'll want to meet you, Mary, especially when I tell him what good friends we are.'

Mary sat back, clearly overwhelmed by the excitement of being introduced to Anderson.

That evening, Eleanor and Mary went to church with their parents. Anderson was one of the few people connected with the Castle who went to the church. The first time he'd appeared everyone had been afraid by his presence, but now he was always there, sitting alone in the first of the makeshift pews.

As Eleanor took Mary up to meet him, Anderson brushed his hair from his eyes and smiled at Eleanor. 'Hello, Eleanor. Did you like your present?'

'Yes,' she said, trying to sound grateful.

Anderson laughed. 'I felt exactly the same way when my parents gave me a dictionary when I was your age. It seems unnecessary, right?'

She didn't want to admit this was exactly what she'd thought.

He turned and took her hand. 'Eleanor, when you're writing stories at school, do you use a dictionary?'

'Sometimes,' she replied, 'but I do my best to get by without it.'

'Why?' Anderson asked.

'I don't know. It seems silly to be checking words all the time.'

'Silly? OK, Eleanor, you're an intelligent girl, right?'

She felt too modest to say 'yes'. 'I'm not sure.'

'Well, take it from me, you're intelligent. And if an intelligent girl like you doesn't know how to spell something, that means it's probably a difficult word. So there's no shame in looking it up, agreed?'

'Agreed.'

'Good. One of the most important lessons anyone has to learn is to ask for help when they need it. Once you've learned that, you'll find your life becomes a lot easier.'

Eleanor considered this, then said, 'Anderson, this is my friend, Mary. She wanted to meet you.'

'Hello, Mary,' said Anderson, 'you're very lucky to have a friend like Eleanor.'

Mary looked as if she were about to faint.

Eleanor could see she was too excited to speak, and leaned in to tell Anderson, 'I'm the lucky one.'

Anderson nodded. 'It's good to have someone you can trust.'

'Oh, I trust Mary more than anyone.' She took a deep breath and then said in a rush, 'Anderson, will Mary be able to come into the Castle with me?'

'Of course, on occasion,' he replied. 'You're allowed to have friends, Eleanor.'

Relieved, Eleanor gave Mary a big hug and tried to pull her away from Anderson. He gently shook Mary's hand, then sat back in the pew and returned his gaze forward, waiting for the service to begin.

'Did you have a nice birthday?' Eleanor's father, Jonathan, asked her that evening, as she was getting ready for bed.

Eleanor knew her father wanted her to say yes, so she nodded and smiled at him. Only when he had left her bedroom did she give this question serious consideration. It had been a quieter birthday than usual, partly because she was getting older, she supposed, but also because her parents seemed unusually distracted, making less of an effort than they usually did. Still, although it had been quiet, this was the first year when she hadn't felt a sense of disappointment that her special day hadn't been quite as exciting as she had hoped. Even at this early age, birthdays were usually bittersweet for Eleanor; but not this year, because for the first time ever, she was looking forward to something even more exciting. As she closed her eyes and waited for sleep to take her, Eleanor thought about Mary and how funny she'd been about Anderson. It was so obvious that she had a crush on him. Eleanor chuckled and buried her head into the soft pillow, vowing that she would never be so silly about any boy she might meet, no matter how handsome he was.

CHAPTER
THREE

On the first day of her training, Anderson came to Eleanor's house just before dawn. Both of Eleanor's parents were still sleeping, and she awoke only because Anderson knocked directly on her bedroom window. Recognising his face through the heavy glass, she opened the window and told him to give her two minutes and she'd come round to the front door. Dressing quickly, she went through the house and let him in.

'Anderson,' she said, 'it's so early.'

He put a finger to his lips. 'I know, and don't worry, I won't wake your parents. But it's time for you to come to the Castle with me.'

'OK,' she said, 'I'll just leave a note.'

She found a pen and left a message for her parents, telling them where she had gone. Then she followed Anderson outside.

He had his white horse with him and told her, 'Go on, don't be afraid. Climb on.'

Eleanor grabbed hold of the stirrups and hoisted herself onto the back of the horse. Anderson climbed up in front of her and cracked the reins down on his horse's flank. The horse started off at a fast gallop, frightening Eleanor, who wasn't used to riding.

Anderson reached behind himself and wrapped an arm round her, saying, 'Don't worry, Eleanor, it's perfectly safe. Soon you'll have a horse of your own and be riding every day.'

Eleanor didn't reply. It was beginning to get light and all around them a chorus of birds was making a tremendous noise. After they had ridden together for a while, they drew closer to the Castle, and Anderson steered his horse towards the stables. He stopped when they reached the stable boy, jumping down and handing him the reins before helping Eleanor dismount.

Although the Castle was at the centre of the community, few ventured inside it, apart from on special occasions. The village grew out from the Castle, with the small, primitive houses of the community surrounding the tall, square, stone construction. It had only one keep, magnificent in size. Inside the keep were several banqueting rooms and accommodation for many more than chose to live there. Eleanor had often wondered about this arrangement, but had never felt confident enough to raise this question with her teachers.

They walked through the arched stone doorway and into the bailey. There was a spiral staircase just inside the entrance, and Anderson immediately started climbing it, instructing Eleanor to follow him. They went up to the third level, and then Anderson directed Eleanor towards a large candlelit room.

There were six people waiting for her. Anderson pointed to the four women standing in front of a large red and white tapestry. 'Eleanor, I'd like you to meet Alexandra, Sarah, Lucinda and Katharine. These are the female members of the Castle Seven.' He then pointed to the two men sitting at a large wooden table. 'And these are the men, Robert and Zoran.'

Zoran raised his hand and waved at her. The others remained still, watching Anderson.

'Eleanor,' said Anderson, 'I've brought you here slightly earlier than the rest of your group because we wanted a chance to speak to you on your own. First, I have to give you a bit of background information. As you are probably already aware, as far as anyone knows, since the fall of the kingdom, there are thirty-nine communities within this country, and each one is based around a different castle.'

Alexandra stepped forward and took up the story. 'Most of these castles are too far away for us to visit them, and no one is sure what might happen in some of them. But we have business and social dealings with the four nearest castles, and we are hoping to expand our travelling and visit further afield. For the moment, however, we must focus our efforts on maintaining our relationship with the nearest communities. It has recently come to the Castle Seven's attention that many of the nearby castles have a group of children who are encouraged to take part in social activity. We need a similar group to take with us when we visit our neighbours, the Greengrove Community. Those chosen will be educated to be able to talk to adults, to play music, to be charming and make a good impression. You were the first girl chosen and we've decided to make you the unofficial leader of the group. The others won't know that you enjoy a special relationship with us, and we'd prefer it if you didn't tell them. We're not asking you to spy on the others, but if someone's unhappy or you think there's a problem, we'd appreciate it if you told us in time for us to do something about it.'

'OK,' said Eleanor.

'Good,' said Anderson. 'Now, most of the time you'll be taught by either Alexandra or me, although all seven of us will take part in your education in one way or another. I know you're a loyal friend, and daughter, and we will never ask you to do anything that you believe is wrong, but from now on you must place your trust in us totally, OK? We will teach you lots of things that you cannot share with anyone, even your closest friends, no matter what.'

'I understand,' said Eleanor, 'you can trust me.'

'I know,' replied Anderson, 'that's why we chose you.'

Eleanor looked round the assembled group. All four women were in their twenties. Alexandra had fine, honey-coloured hair, blue eyes and a mysterious smile. She was wearing a loosely fitting red dress, with intricate stitching around the large, baggy cuffs. It came right up to her neck, and was tightly buttoned at the collar. Eleanor thought Alexandra looked friendly, and felt pleased that of all the women she would be the one teaching her. Alongside Alexandra, Sarah looked slightly more reserved, with hazel eyes and an expression of deep serenity. Sarah wore a white dress with a grey sleeveless tunic buttoned over it. She was the tallest of the four women, and, like Alexandra, seemed aloof from the other two. There was something about their presence that Eleanor found immediately reassuring.

Lucinda and Katharine had taken advantage of Anderson's speech to sit at the table with the two other men. Lucinda wore a pink dress that Eleanor thought was beautiful. Although she wished to be friends with Alexandra and Sarah, she wanted to be dressed like Lucinda. Her outfit was simpler than Alexandra's or Sarah's, and more revealing. She had loose brown hair, bushy and slightly wild. Her physicality was apparent just from looking at her, and she seemed strong and untamed.

Compared to Lucinda, Katharine looked extraordinarily composed. She wore a red and brown patterned dress with a thick black belt, and her hair was neat, shoulder-length and jet black. She was the only woman among the group towards whom Eleanor immediately felt wary, although she didn't know why. She had an instinctive sense that Katharine wasn't really interested in her. She was fingering the ends of her hair in a distracted way and smiling coyly at Anderson. Both Zoran and Robert looked younger than Anderson, more like overgrown boys than fully adult males. The two men wore a similar uniform: black leather tunics with coarse brown trousers.

Zoran's tunic had a silver and ivory engraving of an elephant's head, Robert's a brass bear. They had similar thick, curly hair, although Robert's was blond while Zoran's was brown.

'When will the others be here?' Eleanor asked.

Anderson looked at his watch. 'Robert and Zoran will go and collect them any minute. Alexandra, will you take Eleanor down to the breakfast room?'

Alexandra nodded, and came over to Eleanor. She took her by the shoulder and walked her back to the spiral staircase. They went down two flights of stairs and then Alexandra let Eleanor into another large room, similar to the one they had just left. At the end of the room, a woman wearing a white uniform stood in front of a wooden counter.

'Eleanor,' said Alexandra, 'would you like something to drink while we wait for the others?'

'Just water, please.'

Alexandra nodded and the white-uniformed woman went out through the back door into the kitchen. Eleanor sat at the nearest table. Her teacher took the space beside her.

'This must all feel a little intimidating.'

'It's OK,' said Eleanor. 'It's exciting more than anything else.'

This seemed to please Alexandra. 'I can see we're going to be great friends, you and I.'

The first to come into the breakfast room was an overweight teenage boy with soft, pudgy cheeks, black hair and a sad, disappointed manner. He was followed by two girls. There was something unusual about them, and as Eleanor looked closely, she realised they were twins. Behind them was a second boy. He was tall, lean and seemed cautious, sniffing the air as if this were the only way he could tell whether it was safe to come into the room. He might've been handsome, if it wasn't for his spots, greasy blond hair and thick glasses. Although the twins were both extremely pretty, Eleanor felt slightly less excited about being chosen for the group now she had seen who else had been selected. She also no longer felt scared, noticing that everyone else seemed just as nervous as she'd been before coming in earlier. They looked as if they had only recently been stolen from their beds, heads still full of dreams and sleepiness.

Alexandra stood up. 'OK, everyone, sit down, and wait for your breakfast. Those of you who don't know one another say hello and make your introductions.'

She left them alone in the breakfast room. They crowded around Eleanor at her wooden table. The twins sat on the bench opposite her, both offering the same friendly smile and saying simultaneously:

Hephzibah: 'I'm Hephzi and this is Beth.'

Beth: 'I'm Beth and this is Hephzibah.'

'I'm Eleanor,' she replied.

'Hi, Eleanor,' they chorused. Beth was slightly smaller that Hephzibah, with a bigger nose and shorter hair. Both were wearing blue pinafore dresses over cream shirts. She could tell the twins probably hadn't had much more experience than her of dealing with boys their age, and said in a brave voice, 'And what are your names?'

'I'm Stefan,' replied the taller boy.

'And I'm Michael,' added the other. 'I'm sorry, which one of you is Beth and which is Hephzi?'

They introduced themselves again, before saying, 'Don't worry, we won't be cross if you get us muddled up.'

'Everyone does sometimes,' said Hephzi.

'Even our parents,' admitted Beth.

'But we promise never to play tricks on you.'

'Unless it helps on one of our secret missions.'

The mention of 'secret missions' excited everyone around the table. Eleanor found herself wondering how the others had found out they'd been chosen for this group. She had never seen any of them before, although at school she only really interacted with her own age group and it seemed likely that Stefan and Michael were at least a year older than her, and Hephzibah and Beth a year younger. She hadn't really thought about the selection process until now, and found herself wondering whether their teachers had played a part in deciding who should be part of the team. She also wondered whether Anderson had gone round to all the others' homes, or if Alexandra had been the one to recruit the boys.

'Does anyone know when we'll go on our first mission?' asked Stefan.

'I think it might be quite soon,' said Eleanor. 'Although I suppose we need to do a lot of training first.'

'I can't wait,' said Stefan, 'I've always wanted to travel.'

After they'd eaten breakfast, Anderson reappeared to take the group down to the stables. When Eleanor had thought about what being at the Castle might be like, she'd assumed that some days might be boring, and others exciting, just like school. But so far, she'd had a great time. The Castle Seven had singled her out for special kindness, and even if she wasn't sure about Michael and Stefan, she felt comfortable with the group and thought that the boys were probably too shy to be horrible to her. And she couldn't believe she was getting her own horse so quickly.

The minute she reached the stables Eleanor knew which horse she wanted. Four of the horses were fully grown, but there was a younger, completely white one on the far side of the stable. In her dreams Eleanor was always riding a white horse, and she associated this image with escape and freedom. But Anderson directed her instead to the first horse they came to, which was big and grey with a thick, healthy mane. Hephzi was given the white horse, and a stable boy started to explain how to groom and care for the animals. Beth noticed Eleanor's disappointment and asked her what was wrong.

'It's OK,' she said, 'I'm being silly.'

'No, Eleanor, tell me. What is it?'

23

'I just wanted a different horse, that's all.'

'The white one?' she asked.

Ashamed, Eleanor nodded.

Beth said, 'Don't worry, it's OK. I'll ask my sister. She won't mind.'

Beth rushed around the horses and checked with Hephzi, who was happy to trade horses, but Anderson stepped in.

'Eleanor, I think your horse will be too big for Hephzi. And too headstrong.'

'It's OK,' said Hephzi, 'I really don't mind.'

Anderson looked at Eleanor. 'This is your horse.' He turned to the stable boy. 'What's his name?'

'Nathaniel.'

'Nathaniel, right.' Anderson walked back to the grey horse and ran a hand across his head. 'Eleanor, animals have feelings, just like people. Imagine how you would feel if someone didn't like you because of the way you looked.'

'It's not the way he looks,' Eleanor protested. 'I know it's silly. It's just in my dreams I'm always riding a white horse.'

'I understand, Eleanor, but sometimes things aren't the way you dream them. Nathaniel is your horse. And you'll soon grow to love him.'

'I know,' she said, 'I'm sorry.'

'It's OK, Eleanor. You don't have to apologise.'

Eleanor nodded, and walked back to Nathaniel, hoping she hadn't hurt his feelings.

CHAPTER FOUR

They weren't allowed to go for a ride that morning. They had a busy day, and now they had been introduced to their horses, it was time for the lessons to begin. Alexandra took them for a class that seemed designed mainly to find out what they were doing in school, and balancing their different abilities. Eleanor found that she was equal to the boys, and further on than the twins, although Alexandra explained that, unlike school, where they had usually competed against one another, here they would almost always be working in a group. Eleanor asked if she would still get to write stories, and Alexandra said there would be little time for that, but that her life would soon become so exciting that she wouldn't notice the loss.

As Eleanor was leaving the classroom, Alexandra called her back in. 'How are you finding things?'

'OK.'

'You know, Eleanor, I think you're very brave. I can't imagine how I would've responded if this had happened to me when I was your age. I realise you're probably worried about whether you'll live up to what we expect from you. But, trust me, this is an opportunity that'll change your life for ever. I don't know if Anderson told you this, but one day all of those chosen will get the opportunity to join the Castle Seven, as long as they have remained true to the cause. So, just think, Eleanor, one day you'll be like me, teaching someone else all the things you've learned.'

'Alexandra, how did you become one of the Castle Seven?'

She smiled. 'Eleanor, in life, you'll soon find that nothing is simple. Behind every group, there's another group. Behind every powerful person, there is another, even more powerful person controlling their behaviour. It's been this way for thousands of years. Before the fall of the kingdom it was easier to see who was in control, but now . . . who knows? Some people simply accept that this is the way of the world; others go mad trying to challenge this structure. But, Eleanor, the truth is everyone, somewhere along the line, is given the chance to prove himself or herself.'

Eleanor nodded.

'Can I tell you a secret?' asked Alexandra.

'Of course.'

'I've known Anderson since he was a little boy. The two of us were childhood sweethearts. Back then, there was no evidence that he would go on to become such an important person, but I thought he was the kindest boy I'd ever met.' She paused for a moment, gazing at the Castle's walls, then said, 'For some reason, our love for each other has never worked out. It was sad, but there was nothing either of us could do to change the situation. And although we were no longer in love, I never stopped thinking of him, and he never stopped thinking of me. So when he was asked to set up the Castle Seven, I was the first person he thought of.'

'What about the other women? Are they also . . .?'

'Anderson's ex-girlfriends? No. Sarah is the great-great-granddaughter of the last princess before the fall of the kingdom, and one of the few people within the Castle who has some knowledge of how things used to be. Lucinda worked at one of the best inns just outside our community, and has met travellers from many other castles . . .'

'And Katharine?'

'Katharine's not as distant as she seems, Eleanor. She's just a bit awkward around anyone she doesn't know. But in moments of pressure, she can keep everyone together. She's also fiercely loyal to Anderson. And that's one of the most important qualities that someone doing our job can possess.'

Eleanor nodded, and left the classroom.

By far the strangest thing that happened to Eleanor on that first day occurred at lunchtime. The Castle Seven all had strange expressions on their faces as the cook placed large ceramic bowls in front of the children. Eleanor lifted the lid from her bowl, and immediately screamed. Hundreds of wriggling worms had eaten her food. The others at the table lifted the lids from their bowls. Everyone else had been served something similarly disgusting, and they all looked at the Castle Seven, not understanding why they were laughing.

Zoran turned and grinned at them.

Alexandra tried to apologise, but was laughing so hard that she couldn't get out the words. Finally she managed to say, 'Oh dear, that was funny. It was just a little test, that's all. The idea was meant to be that soon we will be visiting many different castles, and some will have customs that might seem extremely strange to you. It's unlikely that you'll ever be served anything quite so unappetising as a bowl of worms, but it's important that you should learn to hide your distaste in polite social situations. Cook, would you bring the proper lunches, please?'

This wasn't the lesson Eleanor learned from the Castle Seven's nasty trick. What she learned instead was that they weren't entirely to be trusted. It was clear now to Eleanor that the Castle Seven weren't proper teachers, and didn't see themselves as restricted by any rules. Zoran was obviously the joker of the group. He was younger than the others, but rather than frown on his childish behaviour, they seemed to encourage it. A shaggy-haired, usually unshaven man, he was a friendly, excitable presence, but it was hard to reconcile his mischievousness with the Castle Seven's supposedly high aims. Only Anderson seemed entirely trustworthy, and his stern expression showed he wasn't at all impressed by this lunchtime trick.

When the cook had replaced their bowls with proper food, they were given their first lesson in table manners and dining etiquette, something all of the Castle Seven seemed to agree was extremely important. Eleanor had been brought up to be polite, but had been raised on simple meals, and couldn't follow the intricate rules about which piece of cutlery to use and which foods she was or wasn't allowed to pick up with her fingers. She supposed it would all become easier with time and practice.

Much of the afternoon was taken up with their first dance lesson. Zoran, Robert and Lucinda played musical instruments, while Anderson, Alexandra and Sarah walked them through various dance steps. Only Katharine didn't take part, although she stayed with them throughout the session. The big embarrassment for everyone was having to pair up with a child of the opposite sex, but as Michael and Stefan chose Hephzi and Beth for their partners, Eleanor spent most of the afternoon being twirled around by Anderson. He was such a good partner that he made her feel much lighter on her feet than she usually did, and when they returned to solo dancing she was shocked to rediscover how clumsy she really was.

After the dance lesson, they returned to the dining room for another meal, before Anderson took her home on his horse.

The early start, combined with the day's excitements, had exhausted Eleanor, and she fell asleep behind Anderson as he rode. Her body was wedged tightly against his, and she woke up when he brought the horse to a halt. Jumping down, he offered Eleanor his hand and helped her dismount.

'Goodnight, Eleanor,' he said, kissing her forehead.

'Goodnight, Anderson,' she replied, watching him as he turned his horse and rode off into the darkness.

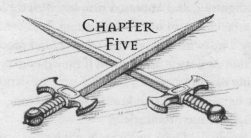

CHAPTER FIVE

The next day began with a sword-fighting lesson. Although Anderson had downplayed the importance of learning this skill when he first talked to Eleanor about what was required of her, it was clear it was a central part of their training programme.

Anderson began by handing out heavy, genuine swords, watching as the children struggled even to lift them above their waists, before collecting them back in and giving each child a wooden replica.

'We'll work on developing those muscles,' he said. 'But the technique is what's important.'

He told them to stand in line, showed them the starting position, and then began talking everyone through the various movements. As he did so, he said, 'Using a sword, like several of the other skills you'll be learning over the next few weeks, is something that you may find you'll never need to put into practice. But it is a discipline that is best learned as early as possible, and you'll find it a useful form of exercise even if you're never in a situation where you're facing an opponent.'

Neither of the boys was much better than Eleanor at sword-fighting, and Anderson diagnosed all three of them as having a problem with finding their centre of gravity. The twins had no such trouble, and proved so adept that Anderson asked them if they'd ever done anything like this before.

'We have play-fights at home,' they told him, 'although we use broomsticks.'

He laughed. 'That's brilliant. You'll be our warriors.'

'OK.' They grinned and bashed their wooden blades together again.

The reward for suffering an hour's painful stretching and waving wooden sticks around was being allowed to take their horses out for the rest of the morning. Eleanor had worried all night about whether Nathaniel would be upset with her about how she'd behaved the day before, and had stolen several sugar lumps from her parents' kitchen as a peace offering. She didn't think Anderson would approve of this, so she kept them tightly wrapped in her sticky hand until she could sneak the horse away from the others when they got outside. Nathaniel didn't seem to bear her any ill will, and happily licked her hand after he'd snaffled up his treat. Although still early, it was beginning to seem as if it would be a warm, pleasant summer's day, and Eleanor was pleased to be outside. She thought of her old school friends and how much more enjoyable this was than being stuck inside a classroom. Today Eleanor felt glad she hadn't got her way about the white horse. He seemed much more temperamental than Nathaniel, rearing and snorting and stamping his hooves, constantly ignoring all poor Hephzi's attempts to keep him under control.

The two boys rode their horses far into the distance of the Castle's gardens, and then slowed them down so they could hover next to each other. Eleanor thought they were probably talking about her and the twins, and she wondered what they were saying. She wished she could confide in the twins in the same way, but they were too excitable, and already had a special bond of their own. She knew Alexandra was keen to develop a friendship with her, but was worried that being too strongly associated with the adults would isolate her from the other children. Eleanor was thinking ahead, and it worried her that when they went on their first visit, the Castle Seven would be spending time with the adults from the other castle and the children would have to fend for themselves. The Castle Seven's lessons seemed to concentrate far too much on the rules of adult interaction, and she was worried that this wouldn't help at all when it came to meeting people of her own age.

'Ah,' said Katharine, when Eleanor voiced this concern during their afternoon conversation lesson, 'you shouldn't worry about that. Besides, what do you suggest? We can hardly teach you how to pull their hair and run away.'

'Will they be like us?' Hephzi asked.

'What do you mean?'

'Will they have been chosen from their community and given the same sort of training?'

'Not exactly. That's partly our weakness and partly our secret weapon,' said Katharine, smiling. 'After the fall of the kingdom, there was a long period when some people travelled about, trying to find others like them. Most of the castles have an equivalent group to us seven, but in many communities they haven't been chosen for their skills, but have inherited the privilege through tradition or their family history. Do you understand what that means?'

They looked blank.

'It means that many children you meet, including those on this first expedition, will be of noble birth and a lot of what we're teaching you will already come naturally to them, but they will probably also be lazy about them and have fallen into bad habits.'

'How will you present us?' asked Eleanor.

Katharine gave her a long, slow look. Eleanor felt intimidated by this appraisal, especially when her teacher said, 'Yes, Eleanor, well done, you've seen through the plan. Most of us aren't of noble birth, but we know enough not to be found out. In some cases, we will be dealing with people like us, or maybe even revolutionary groups who detest privilege and will only talk to us if they think we've overthrown the noblemen of our own Castle. And the whole point of your education and training is to learn how to wear your lessons lightly. We won't be introducing you as children whom we've chosen and trained. We'll say

34

you're a representative selection of the younger members of our community.'

Eleanor nodded, not wanting to get into an argument with Katharine. She could see the logic in what she was saying, but it made her nervous about having given up on her school education. She thought back to what Alexandra had told her about how one day she would be made one of the Castle Seven, and realised it was like getting a job before deciding what she wanted to do. She felt too young to have the rest of her life mapped out, and worried that she would never get to spend time with normal people ever again. More than anything, she missed the safety and security of her lessons at school, which had never had anything to do with the possibility of life outside the community.

Her parents were certainly concerned about what was happening to her. As the weeks went on, she found herself arguing with them more and more, demanding to know why they didn't already know the things she had recently been taught. Anderson and Alexandra had introduced her to a whole new library of books she never knew existed, and had begun to show her the basic grammar of many different languages. She knew she was supposed to wear her learning lightly, but the exciting rush of new knowledge made this almost impossible. She felt angry that so much had been denied to her, and asked her parents why they had never experienced any curiosity beyond the rituals of

35

their daily working lives. This kind of conversation made April angry, but Jonathan struggled to understand, asking his daughter whether there was anything she had learned that she could teach him. She tried her best to open his eyes, but his heart wasn't in it, and every time Eleanor fed him a morsel of the Castle Seven's wisdom, he looked bored and drifted away. Worse still, neither of her parents had taken advantage of being able to spend time in the Castle. The boys' parents behaved in the same way, and Eleanor often talked to them about how frustrating she found this. Only the twins' parents, who were as confident as their offspring, seemed to enjoy a change of life thanks to their children's success, spending every night eating or drinking in the Castle's visitors' hall. Eleanor hoped that one day her parents might enjoy a similar confidence, but knew that no matter how much she wished for this change in their personalities, there was little chance of it ever happening.

CHAPTER
SIX

After two months of training, the Castle Seven told
the children they were going to throw a party where
they could try out all the social skills they had been
taught. All kinds of people from the community had
been invited, including all of their families. The
prospect of being at a party with their parents
mortified Michael and Stefan, but Anderson told them
it was an important test of character.

'Everyone's embarrassed by their family when
they're a teenager,' he told them, 'but the fastest route
to full maturity is to understand that how your parents
behave is no reflection on you. You are all independent
individuals, and other people will accept you in your
own right. Besides, when we visit other castles no one
will even know your parents exist.'

In order to prepare for the party, tailors and
hairdressers came to the Castle to dress and groom the
children. Eleanor's hairdresser was very admiring of
her golden locks, and didn't see the need to do much
beyond removing her split ends with a quick trim. But
her tailor was horrified by her cheap, dowdy clothes,

and insisted that as soon as her new outfits were finished everything she owned must be consigned to the bin.

'Can't I keep anything?' she asked. 'Just in case of emergencies?'

'I'm going to make you seven outfits. That should be enough to keep you going.'

Seven outfits! Eleanor had never had more than three changes of clothes in her entire life. She stood there with her arms outstretched as the tailor took her measurements. Eleanor's eyes grew wide as she watched her roll out lengths of various beautiful fabrics, almost beside herself with excitement at the prospect of having all these outfits designed exclusively for her.

But if Eleanor was happy then, it was nothing compared to a few days later when the tailor returned with the clothes she had made. The two outfits that immediately caught her eye were a pink dress like the one Lucinda had worn on Eleanor's first day in the Castle, and an even more elegant silver gown. She asked the tailor if she could try it on.

'Of course,' she said, turning around while Eleanor undressed.

Eleanor picked up the silver dress and stepped into it, gently gathering the material around herself and waiting while the tailor fastened the buttons. Then she turned and looked in the mirror.

'Oh,' said the tailor, 'you need this.' She went back to her bags of clothes and brought out a long conical hat with a thin stream of lace trailing from the top. Standing behind Eleanor, the tailor placed it on her head.

Eleanor was overcome. 'I look . . . I look like . . . a . . . a . . . princess.'

As soon as she said this word, Eleanor was wrached with guilt. Although this sort of talk wasn't outlawed in the community, she knew that, even within the Castle, it wasn't a good idea to refer to the time before the fall of the kingdom. It would have been acceptable to say this in front of Katharine or Alexandra, but she could see the tailor flinch, and worried that she had offended her.

'I didn't mean . . . it's just . . . so beautiful.'

'It's all right,' said the tailor, 'I was asked to make you look like that. I'm glad you like it.'

'I love it. Oh, thank you, thank you so much.'

'Don't mention it. It's my job.'

The others had similarly dazzling outfits. The morning before the party, they had a dress rehearsal, with the five of them practising conversation with the Castle Seven. Although Michael and Stefan had outfits like Anderson's, what really improved their appearance was what the barbers had done to their hair. Even their teenage skin couldn't spoil their new air of sophistication. Michael had lost some of his puppy fat through the constant exercise, and although he still had doughy cheeks, they made him look cute rather than childish. Eleanor still didn't fancy him or Stefan, but she had noticed the twins giving them increasingly flirtatious looks, and knew they were still trying to decide who should chase which one. What she didn't know was that both twins, being more alike than they would ever admit, fancied Michael, and they were still waiting for him to give a sign as to which girl he preferred.

Eleanor knew the time of their first expedition had to be growing close. The Castle Seven were increasingly excitable, especially Lucinda and Zoran. Eleanor had recently come to the conclusion that Lucinda was in many ways a female version of Zoran. She wasn't quite so keen on silly stunts, but she was younger than the other women, and lacked their calm reserve. During this dress rehearsal, these two talked mainly to the boys, while Eleanor walked off into a quiet corner with Sarah and Alexandra.

'So,' whispered Alexandra to Eleanor, 'how do you think the group's getting on? Is there anything we should know?'

Eleanor shook her head. 'Everyone's excited about our first trip, but that's all.'

Alexandra and Sarah exchanged a glance, but didn't say anything. Eleanor had begun to find Sarah fascinating. Although she barely spoke, whenever she did, her words sounded as if she had been considering them for some time, even if she was answering a question that had only just been asked. Katharine liked to pretend to be mysterious, but Sarah seemed in possession of genuine secrets, and Eleanor was keen to know what they were.

'And do you like your new clothes?' Alexandra asked.

'I love them,' Eleanor replied. 'Thank you so much.'

'Oh, don't thank us. Think of them as a uniform you need for your job.'

Sarah looked at Alexandra. 'You sounded just like my mother then. That was exactly the sort of thing she used to say.'

Alexandra nodded, and changed the subject. Eleanor realised she had just been taught a lesson in discretion.

That night the Castle was decorated more elaborately than it ever had been before, even (although, of course, Eleanor had no memory of this) before the fall of the kingdom. Large flaming torches marked the path to the entrance from almost a mile away, coloured banners were hung from every crenel, and minstrels played music that could be heard from far in the distance. There was no one checking invitations and anyone brave enough to gate-crash could mingle freely with the guests. By and large, the uninvited – most of whom still felt superstitious about anything that happened in the Castle – stayed away, but there were a few brave youths who had the night of their lives. Wine flowed freely, but the underage stuck to water.

Eleanor arrived at the Castle at seven-thirty in the company of her parents. April had been so impressed by Eleanor's silver dress that she worried all day about how plain she would look alongside her daughter. Eleanor guiltily decided not to show her mother the other six outfits she'd been given. Jonathan reassured his wife that it didn't matter how they dressed: the evening wasn't about them, they had been invited as Eleanor's parents and this was reason enough for them to feel proud.

At the moment they joined the queue, Alexandra appeared alongside them, touching Eleanor's arm and asking to be introduced to her parents. After Eleanor had done so, Alexandra said to them, 'You should be very proud of your daughter. She picks things up incredibly quickly.'

'Oh, I know,' said Jonathan, 'she's always been like that. Ever since she was a baby.'

April shot Jonathan a look. He shrugged, as if unable to see any harm in making such an innocuous comment. Eleanor felt embarrassed by how frustrated her parents seemed to get with each other for no obvious reason. The way they behaved was so different to the Castle Seven, who never argued and avoided any possible confrontation, yet still seemed as if they were always being totally honest with one another. Eleanor had hoped that being in the Castle might improve her parents' behaviour, especially when they saw other adults talking normally, but now she knew she would be disappointed.

Alexandra smiled and moved away from them, heading further down the queue to where Eleanor could see Michael standing with his parents.

'She seemed nice,' said Jonathan. 'Is she one of your teachers?'

'Of course she's one of her teachers,' snapped April. 'Who else would she be?'

'They don't call them teachers,' said Eleanor quietly. 'She's one of the Castle Seven.'

The queue was moving quickly, as the people already inside spread further up into the higher levels of the Castle. It was full of adults, and although it was still early, the atmosphere had already begun to feel intimidating. As they made their way into the main hall, Eleanor noticed Katharine and Anderson standing together.

'Anderson!' Eleanor called.

He turned round. 'Good evening, Eleanor. And hello, Mr and Mrs Conway.'

Jonathan was still smarting from his wife's earlier comment, and didn't say anything in reply. April smiled and held out her hand.

'Can I get you all drinks?' asked Anderson.

'That would be lovely,' said April, 'thank you.'

Eleanor's embarrassment and frustration at the beginning of the party soon disappeared as the evening progressed. Anderson rescued all the children, bringing their parents together so they didn't feel isolated. Eleanor saw the point of this arrangement, as the other parents seemed to be very similar to her own. Alexandra rejoined Eleanor's side and deftly transported her up and down the various levels of the Castle, taking her into rooms for conversations with particular people and then moving on before anyone became bored. She noticed Sarah serving a similar purpose with Hephzi, and Lucinda with Beth. The boys were together in the company of Robert and Zoran, who didn't seem as interested in social interaction as in getting the boys to bring them as many glasses of wine as possible. Before long, it was obvious that Zoran was completely drunk.

By midnight, most of the parents had returned home. They'd wanted their children to come with them, but the Castle Seven had refused to allow this, saying that their presence at the party was as important as the daytime training. This angered April and Jonathan, who could see no reason for keeping Eleanor up so late, but the Castle Seven took no notice. Eleanor didn't really understand why they wanted her to stay, especially as most of the guests had already left, and those who were still there were too drunk to remember anyone's name after they'd been introduced. Then Michael came up to her and said, 'Come with me a moment.'

'OK,' she said, following him out onto the battlements, 'what's wrong?'

'Zoran said they're going to make an announcement after the party.'

Eleanor was suddenly worried that the announcement would be that the group hadn't done what was expected of them that evening and would be disbanded.

Instead, Michael said, 'We're going on our first mission the day after tomorrow.'

44

'Are you sure?' she asked. 'He's not just making it up because he's drunk?'

'I don't think so. He sounded fairly certain.'

'I can't believe it,' she said. 'Do you feel ready?'

'Not really. But then again they said this trip should be quite straightforward. It's a castle we've got friendly relations with, and they're only taking us there to show us off. So it should be fine, I think.'

'Yes,' said Eleanor, 'I'm sure you're right.'

Zoran had been telling the truth. In the early hours of the morning, after the Castle had cleared, Anderson made the announcement. In two days' time they would be on their way to visit the Greengrove Community.

CHAPTER
SEVEN

They rode out. It would take them three days and two nights to reach the Greengrove Community's castle. On this first day they set out just before dawn, having packed the night before. They wanted to leave under cover of darkness, Anderson told Eleanor, to minimise fuss in the community. Hardly anyone showed up to see them off, with only the twins' parents and a few curious friends prepared to arise so early. The twins' parents were almost as excitable as the twins themselves, and Eleanor found them far too loud for this time in the morning. So she kept out of their way, and waited for them to leave.

The plan was to ride to an inn just outside the borders of their community in time for an early breakfast. Eleanor was still having trouble with these very early starts, especially after having to stay up so late two nights before. There had been an edge of desperation to their exercises yesterday, as the Castle Seven made the group run through everything they'd learned one more time. Eleanor sensed that the Castle Seven were being slightly dishonest, downplaying the potential dangers awaiting them, and she was convinced there was definitely something about the Greengrove Community that frightened them.

The twelve riders divided into smaller groups as they started galloping. Eleanor was at the front, riding alongside Anderson and Alexandra. The pace they set was almost too fast for her, and she held on as tight as she could, terrified of falling. There was something dreamlike about riding Nathaniel in the near darkness. Eleanor had no sense of what awaited her, even outside the borders of their community, let alone when they reached this other community. Riding took it out of her physically, and although Anderson promised they would take lots of breaks, she worried she wasn't up to such a long trip. No matter how much they had practised in the Castle grounds, it was a completely different experience to travelling over unfamiliar land.

They rode for almost two hours before they reached the inn. Watching the sun come up relieved Eleanor of much of her tiredness; and as she started to relax, her muscles eased into a more comfortable position and riding Nathaniel began to feel much less painful. She could feel the horse adjusting his rhythm beneath her, and as the inn came into view, Anderson and Alexandra began to slow their own horses, waiting for the others, who were spread over a distance of half a mile.

The inn looked quiet and Eleanor asked Anderson, 'Are you sure it's open?'

'Yes. It's just early, that's all. We planned it this way to avoid the morning rush.'

The first person to come alongside them was Lucinda. 'Ah,' she said, 'I see nothing's changed.'

'This is where Lucinda used to work,' Anderson explained, 'before she came to us.'

Lucinda looked at Anderson, and then gave her horse one final kick, riding down to the inn.

'If you want to go with her,' Alexandra told Anderson and Eleanor, 'I'm happy to wait for the others.'

'I do feel tired,' said Eleanor, 'and could do with a break.'

'Already?' asked Anderson, and then he smiled. 'No, don't worry, I understand. You'll soon get used to it.'

They rode behind Lucinda down to the inn. There was a place to tie their horses safely, and Anderson helped Eleanor with this before going inside. Lucinda was in the midst of receiving a huge hug from a man wearing an apron over his brown clothes.

'My girl,' he said, 'you've come back to me.'

'Is that her dad?' Eleanor whispered to Anderson.

He shook his head. 'Her boss.'

'Are these your friends?' asked the innkeeper.

'Yes,' she said, 'that's Anderson and that's Eleanor. There are nine others coming behind us.'

'Wow,' he said, 'so what's the occasion?'

Lucinda explained, and the innkeeper asked her, 'You're one of the Castle Seven?'

She nodded. 'Have you heard of us?'

'Of course. My dear girl, I had no idea you'd done so well for yourself.' He squinted at Anderson. 'You're

48

one of them too, aren't you? I remember you coming in here before.'

Before he could answer, the door opened and Katharine came through with Stefan. She looked annoyed. Eleanor thought she was cross with Anderson, and then dismissed this possibility from her mind. The Castle Seven didn't get angry with one another. She was probably just tired from all the riding.

The innkeeper directed them towards a long wooden table.

'There's water there. I'll start cooking your breakfasts.'

Eleanor sat opposite Lucinda. 'How long did you work here?'

'Seven years. I started when I was about your age.'

This shocked Eleanor, who couldn't imagine working in an inn. She'd never even been inside one before. She recognised the smell of beer, soon couldn't smell anything else, and became worried this would put her off her food.

The rest of the group slowly began to arrive. Michael looked exhausted, and sat down as quickly as he could, pouring himself a cup of cold water and drinking it back.

'The children are finding this hard,' Katharine told Anderson. 'Maybe we should slow down.'

Anderson shook his head. 'We can take longer breaks, but we need to keep up the pace. The Greengrove Community expect us to show up on time. If we don't manage to do that, we give them the advantage, and you know how difficult that will make things. Besides, we don't want them to think we're rude.'

Katharine nodded, and looked away.

The innkeeper made them a fine breakfast, with plates of bacon and sausage balanced with big bowls of fruit. Lucinda had told him they had a long ride ahead of them, and he did his best to give them food that would boost their energy. Everyone ate hungrily, and the innkeeper expressed amazement at how much food they managed to get through.

After breakfast, the innkeeper sat down with Anderson, and Eleanor listened as they swapped travellers' tales. Anderson noticed Eleanor's eavesdropping and had to keep reminding the innkeeper to leave out the most disturbing parts of his stories. They were given a while to rest and then the innkeeper returned to the kitchen to tell his chef to make picnic lunches for the whole group.

'We won't be going to another inn for lunch?' Eleanor asked Anderson.

He shook his head. 'There isn't one. We'll be travelling mainly through wilderness today and tomorrow. We should reach the next inn tomorrow night. But we'll be camping tonight.'

'What about dinner?'

'Don't worry, we have provisions. But they need to be cooked. We'll build a big fire tonight. I promise you it'll be OK, Eleanor. Better than OK: it'll be fun.'

Eleanor nodded, and went outside to join the others. The twins were playing together, chasing each other and scuffing up huge clouds of dust.

'Isn't this exciting?' Hephzi asked Eleanor. 'I can't believe we're going into the wilderness. I mean, I knew that would be part of it, but now it's actually happening, don't you think it's so terribly exciting?'

'Yes,' said Eleanor, not wanting them to see she was afraid. Whenever anyone had talked to her about the wilderness before, they had always made it sound terrifying. There were things in the wilderness: scary animals, wolves. Being in the darkness with only canvas for protection was a really frightening idea.

Eleanor felt a hand on her shoulder. She turned round and saw Michael, who said, 'I'm afraid, too.'

She was so relieved to hear this that she gave him a hug, then jumped back quickly in case the twins had witnessed this and thought she was trying to move in on the boy they liked.

They stayed at the inn until the sun was high in the sky and the inn's regular patrons had begun to arrive. The innkeeper wished them luck and they rode out. This time, Eleanor decided she didn't want to be at the front of the pack, and instead joined the middle of the group, in a small cluster with Sarah and Lucinda. The three of them didn't talk much, and the only constant noise was the sound of the horses' hooves beating on the ground beneath them.

Eleanor had always assumed the wilderness would live up to its name and be an overgrown garden. She thought they would have to hack their way through unkempt greenery, but in reality it wasn't that different to the grounds of their own community. There were places that were a bit difficult to get through, but Anderson led them down paths that seemed well trodden and maintained. Eleanor shouted across to Sarah about this, and she replied, 'Yes, well, there are plenty of people who live in the wilderness, you know. In spite of everything you've probably been told at home and school, not everyone wants to live in a community.'

Eleanor didn't like Sarah's tone, and wondered why she had answered her innocent question so crossly. She had never been taught about life outside the community, and thought that this should have been part of the training given to them by the Castle Seven.

'Things will get more difficult as we go on, though, Eleanor. We're still not too far into the wilderness.'

They continued to ride. Eleanor didn't see any people or houses, and wondered how many individuals really did choose to live in the wilderness. She imagined the people who lived outside the community probably didn't have families. How could they get by without schools or churches? Those who lived in this area could go to the inn to meet other people, but further out there was nothing but countryside. They probably hunted for their food, but what happened if they got sick, or ran out of money? Eleanor felt glad her parents had chosen to live within a community.

Several hours later, they stopped next to a stream to have their lunch. The twins asked if they could paddle in the water, and Anderson laughed and told them that would be fine. They ate their lunches quickly, stripped off their shoes and socks and began playing in the water. The Castle Seven refrained from joining them, but watched in amusement. Eleanor steered clear of the twins – who, as usual, were being far too boisterous, happily splashing around, kicking, and trying to start a water-fight – and headed further downstream with Michael.

'It's OK so far, isn't it?' he asked Eleanor.

She nodded. 'Yeah. Although it's tonight I'm worried about.'

'Me too,' he replied. 'I've never slept outdoors before, but my dad did once. He wasn't travelling or anything, he'd just quarrelled with his parents and run away from home. He had a tent but he said it was still terrifying, just all the noise of nature at night. Owls and all kinds of other creatures stirring in the night. He said that animals are different in the wilderness. They're used to having no humans around and do all kinds of strange things.'

Eleanor shivered. 'Wolves.'

'Are there wolves in the wilderness?' he asked.

She nodded. 'That's where they live.'

Michael looked hard at her. She could see she was scaring him, and felt guilty. She'd wanted him to give her reassurance, but saw he was too nervous, and realised she would have to calm him. 'They won't find us, though. And even if they do, the Castle Seven will protect us, won't they?'

'Yeah,' he said, 'they must be used to dealing with wolves.'

After an hour's rest, the Castle Seven told everyone to get out of the stream. Alexandra handed Eleanor a towel and said, 'It's important to dry yourself properly. Especially when you're out here in the wilderness. We can't risk any of you getting ill.'

Eleanor nodded, and followed Alexandra back to the horses. Nathaniel didn't look tired at all, but rather as if he were pleased finally to be free of the restriction of the stables. He was an obedient horse, and Eleanor was pleased that Anderson had insisted that she rode him on that first morning of training. It had been a valuable lesson for her, even though she still dreamed of riding the white horse. Alexandra helped her climb onto Nathaniel's back, and as soon as everyone else was on their horse, Anderson drew them all into a circle.

'OK,' he said, 'I appreciate that you're all feeling tired. I had forgotten how exhausting I found my first proper ride because it was so many years ago, and I should've spent some time getting you used to travelling over longer distances. But I'm afraid we can't turn back.

'From now on, we're going to be moving much more slowly, through extremely difficult terrain. The

Castle Seven may separate during this journey, and we may try different routes. But I don't want any of you children doing this. It's important that you are in sight of at least one of the Castle Seven at all times. Is that understood?'

They nodded.

'Good,' said Anderson. 'Eleanor, you ride up front with me.'

Anderson turned and kicked his horse, heading for a bank of extremely tall wild grass. Eleanor went after him, and tried to stay close as he twisted and turned, changing paths with ever-increasing frequency.

'Is Michael OK?' he asked her.

'What do you mean?'

'He's afraid, isn't he?'

'No more than me.'

'What are you afraid of?'

'Being in the wilderness. And wolves.'

Anderson laughed. 'I won't lie to you, Eleanor. This is a dangerous journey. But you mustn't be afraid. The thing is, you probably don't realise just how well your training has prepared you. You can cope in any situation, even if you don't realise it yet. Take the sword-fighting. Until you're actually in a situation where you're forced to pull your sword, you won't truly believe you've got that skill. But when a human being is in danger, and they know they're in danger, something extraordinary happens to them which gives them strength they never knew they had. It's a chemical reaction that takes place within the body, and as long as you have those basic skills, your adrenalin will help you meet your full potential. And the truth is, Eleanor, as much as I want to protect you, the reality is that now you've chosen this path, you'll probably find that one day you have to face all your greatest fears.'

Eleanor understood what Anderson was telling her, but there was something about his tone that made her nervous. It was as if he *wanted* her to be in a dangerous situation, to see if she would react in a way that would make him proud. Once again, Eleanor felt a creeping sensation that she had been given a destiny she didn't desire.

Anderson hadn't been exaggerating the difficulty of the next part of their journey. But, although it was physically more draining, Eleanor enjoyed this change of rhythm. She preferred the slow movement forward to the constant thunder of her horse's hooves. It was much more peaceful, and she took the opportunity to talk to Anderson. Every so often, the greenery would become so thick that Anderson would have to dismount and slash through it with his sword before they could move forward. After he had done this many times, he turned to Eleanor, passed her his sword, and said, 'Now you try.'

In spite of all her training, Eleanor still found wielding a sword hard, although she was satisfied when each swooping motion hacked a space for them to move through. As she did this, she found herself wanting to confide something to Anderson that she knew she shouldn't say. It was her friend's secret, and she knew her friend would be upset with her for revealing it. But she trusted Anderson, and wanted to tell him.

'Anderson,' she said, 'you remember my friend Mary, the one who came up with me when we met you in church.'

'Vaguely,' he replied.

'Oh,' she said, disappointed. 'Well, she's got a huge crush on you.'

Anderson looked at Eleanor. 'Why are you telling me this?'

'I don't know. I thought you might be flattered.'

'Flattered?' he said with a laugh. 'That a little girl I don't even know has a schoolgirl crush on me? Don't be silly, Eleanor.'

Eleanor felt embarrassed, but also cross. She should have known that was how Anderson would react. He could be so serious sometimes. And now it had turned out not to mean anything to him, she felt guilty about revealing Mary's secret. Filled with mixed emotions, she came forward and started hacking again. Anderson waited until she had stopped and then took the sword from her.

'Enough,' he said, 'I think you've got the hang of it now.'

They continued their journey until long after it was dark. Just as Eleanor was ready to drop from exhaustion, Anderson found a large patch of relatively flat land and suggested this was the perfect place to pitch their tents.

Although she was desperate for a rest, Anderson got her to help him unpack the bags on the back of his horse. Eleanor was becoming fed up with Anderson, and was looking forward to the arrival of the rest of their group. Alexandra was the next to show up, and she was clearly drained from an afternoon with the twins. As more people arrived, putting up the tents became much easier.

When the three tents were erected, the group had to decide who would sleep where. Four of the Castle Seven – Sarah, Katharine, Anderson and Lucinda – didn't want to sleep with the children, so they had the first tent to themselves. Robert and Zoran went in with the two boys. That left Alexandra to share the third tent with Eleanor and the twins. As soon as this arrangement was agreed, Zoran led the children off to search for dry wood to build a fire. Eleanor was so tired she could barely move, but Zoran's enthusiasm for this task was infectious, and she was soon enjoying the search. After they'd collected enough wood, they built a large fire, and Zoran showed them how to light it safely. Alexandra and Anderson produced the night's provisions from their bags, including beans, potatoes and huge chunks of meat, and then started to cook their dinner. Zoran had brought a huge flagon of cider with him, and he and Robert started to drink it, while the rest of the Castle Seven drank wine. The children had water.

After they'd eaten dinner, everyone crawled into their tent to sleep. Eleanor could hear Zoran telling the boys a bedtime story in their tent, but found it hard to hear the words. She knew it must have been a funny story, though, because every couple of minutes Stefan and Michael burst into laughter. Before long, the story finished and the only sound Eleanor could hear before she finally dropped off was Zoran snoring.

The pounding of a horse's hooves was a constant sound in Eleanor's dreams, and once again she pictured herself riding, only this time she was completely alone. She was back on the white horse, and in her heart she knew that something terrible had happened, although she had no idea what it was. The dream became increasingly frightening as the skies darkened, and suddenly she heard a terrible scream.

As she awoke, she realised the scream was real. Jumping up before anyone else had a chance to wake, Eleanor ran out of her tent and saw a dark grey shape by the side of the boys' tent. Immediately, she knew what it was. Just as Anderson had warned her that afternoon, sooner or later she would have to face all her greatest fears.

The wolf had bitten through the side of the boys' tent and then sunk his teeth into the first thing that looked like food. This was Stefan's leg. His scream and sudden movements had distracted the wolf, and stopped him doing too much harm, although there were large, bloody bite marks on Stefan's thigh. Now the wolf had frozen, but Eleanor was worried that he might be getting ready to attack again. She could see the wolf's breath rising from its mouth and flinched as he opened his jaws, a mess of blood and thick saliva dripping from his yellow teeth. Eleanor's heart was beating so fast she thought she would vomit. Suddenly, something snapped inside her and she ran back inside her tent to retrieve her sword. She was ready to kill the wolf before letting him hurt any of her friends, but didn't want to encourage him to leap at her if there was a safer way of resolving the situation. She could see she'd got the wolf's attention, so, instead of stabbing him, she started to walk backwards slowly into the darkness, almost urging the wolf to follow.

The wolf watched Eleanor for a moment, then lunged straight at her. She screamed and fell back, and felt his fur brush over her bare leg as he disappeared into the night.

Anderson immediately came over to Eleanor and took the sword from her.

'Eleanor,' he shouted, 'are you OK?'

She nodded. 'He didn't hurt me. He was too afraid. But he hurt Stefan.'

Anderson turned back and saw that Stefan had passed out from the pain and shock of the wolf attack. Everyone in the camp was surrounding his tent. Eleanor watched in surprise as Sarah looked up to the skies and shouted, 'I knew this trip was a mistake. This expedition is doomed.'

Anderson shouted at her, 'Sarah, not in front of the children. And please, don't get worked up. The boy is OK. Zoran, try to bring him round. Lucinda, fetch the medical supplies. You'll have to be the nurse tonight.'

She nodded, and ran to the horses, who had been equally disturbed by the commotion. Eleanor returned to her tent. It took them an hour to treat Stefan's leg and make sure he was still able to walk, and, more importantly, ride. By this time, Eleanor, in spite of the excitement, was absolutely exhausted and in desperate need of sleep. Before all of this, when she was restless and bored at home, she had often longed for adventure, but now she found it was almost too much to bear. Sarah's earlier comment had been unsettling, but Eleanor tried not to think about what it might have meant and longed for morning, when she was sure everyone would have calmed down.

CHAPTER
EIGHT

Eleanor's predictions had been correct, and the following morning everyone seemed much calmer. Stefan's leg was bandaged, and he didn't appear to have any trouble getting around. The night's disruption meant that they all slept late the following morning, and they ate their breakfast quickly before remounting their horses and beginning the second day of their journey. The riding was much easier, as they headed to the top of a huge ravine. It was hotter than the day before, which made them go slower, but also made the travelling more pleasant.

Eleanor rode alongside Sarah, and asked her, 'What did you mean last night when you said this trip was doomed?'

'Oh, I'm sorry, Eleanor. Anderson was right, I shouldn't have said that in front of you.'

'Yes, but what did you mean by it?'

'Nothing. I was being silly. I've just been having some nightmares about it, that's all.'

'Really?' Eleanor asked. 'Because I've been having nightmares, too.'

'Yes, Eleanor, but that's different.'

'No, it's not,' she said. 'These aren't like normal nightmares. They're really specific.'

'What happens?' Sarah asked.

'I'm riding the white horse, but I'm all on my own, and something terrible has happened. That's the dream I had last night. But before that I dreamed of a wolf, just like last night. And a skeleton.'

Sarah laughed. 'Well, my dream's nothing like that. It's just a standard dream of being trapped somewhere. It's nothing spectacular. I've had the dream ever since I was your age. It's only because I'm scared of the dark.'

Eleanor nodded. 'I thought only children were scared of the dark.'

'Well, now you know. Some adults are, too.'

Eleanor had the impression that Sarah didn't want to continue this conversation. They were reaching a point along the top of the ravine where there was only enough room for one horse at a time, and she let Sarah go in front of her, following behind. They were only about ten feet away from a very steep drop, and Eleanor realised that her life depended on Nathaniel keeping his footing. She leaned down and whispered to him, 'Good boy, you look after me, OK?'

They didn't stop for lunch until early afternoon. Anderson had promised everyone that if they kept up the pace they could have more time to themselves when they reached the next inn. 'I've been to this place before,' he told them. 'It has all kinds of luxuries.

Including a bathroom. Everyone who wants one can have a hot bath tonight.'

'Does it have a bar?' asked Zoran.

'Yes, Zoran, it has a bar. But I don't want you getting drunk and losing all your money at poker tonight. We still have another day of travelling after this.'

Zoran smiled broadly. 'They have poker?'

Michael sat down next to Eleanor to eat his lunch. 'How's Stefan?' she asked.

'He's OK. Thanks to you. It was very brave of you to rescue him last night. He knows that wolf could have hurt him much more badly if it wasn't for you.'

Eleanor shook her head. 'I don't think so. He was just hungry. I don't think he wanted to hurt Stefan.'

'Still, I couldn't have done it. And I thought you were scared of wolves, too?'

'I am,' she said, 'they terrify me. But it's different now I've seen a real one.'

He nodded. 'Eleanor, what do you think they'll be like?'

'At this castle? Well, I think they'll be more used to meeting people than we are. But I think they want us to impress the adults more than the other kids.'

'What if they're horrible?'

'They won't be. Not if their parents are there. And if they are, we'll just have to be horrible, too.'

There was a renewed enthusiasm among the group during the afternoon's travelling. Everyone was keen to reach the inn, and Anderson realised that he'd underestimated how far they had come. If they kept going at the same pace, they would get there by five o'clock. As they drew closer to the inn, more people started to appear, and Eleanor asked if they were nearing a community.

'No,' said Anderson, 'but this is a good midpoint for many travellers. Some communities aren't as restrictive as ours, and the idea of travelling isn't as frightening to the people who live in them. In fact, in several communities people go travelling just for fun.'

'Why aren't the people in our community like that?' she asked.

'It's all down to their experiences after the fall of the kingdom. Our people had a hard time, and they thought they'd never be able to rebuild anything. We're a very small community, and vulnerable to attack. Some people understand that the best way to avoid this is to foster bonds with other castles, but others believe that as long as we're quiet and keep ourselves to ourselves, no one will decide to invade us.'

They reached the inn, and stopped outside to tie up the horses. Zoran leaped off his horse and ran into the bar. Anderson tapped Robert on the shoulder and said, 'Keep an eye on him, will you?'

Robert nodded and followed Zoran. Everyone else went up to look at their rooms. Eleanor had to share hers with the twins, but she didn't mind, and all three were excited about sleeping in a room together. The twins immediately started jumping up and down on the bed.

'This is fantastic, isn't it?' they chorused. 'Our own room.'

'Yes,' said Eleanor, 'it'll be nice to sleep in a bed.'

She went across to the bed in the corner of the room and sat down. Taking off her boots, she tested the mattress. Next to the bed was a scary-looking wooden man. It looked like a mummy, only with a frightening face. It had a black moustache, piercing eyes and a large red nose. Eleanor wasn't sure she wanted to sleep alongside it, but the twins had already taken the other two beds, which were next to each other, and she knew she wouldn't be able to persuade them to swap.

Eleanor had worn the same outfit, a dark blue dress that was the least elegant of the seven the tailor had made for her, throughout the last two days, and now that she had the chance, she was eager to wash and change. Remembering Anderson's promise that everyone could have a hot bath when they reached the inn, she decided to try to slip quietly in there first. Searching through her bags, she found a towel, and then sneaked out of her room, heading down the corridor to the bathroom. It was empty, so she quickly ran inside.

Lying in the bathtub, Eleanor thought about her parents. It was the first time she'd contemplated how far she had come – not just the physical distance, but also the emotional experiences she'd had – in the time since Anderson had chosen her. Since confronting the wolf, she had realised the truth of what Anderson had

66

told her about how there were many lessons she'd learned but wouldn't truly understand until she had the chance to put them into practice. She was a cautious girl, and didn't want things to turn out badly if that could be avoided, but this was supposed to be an adventure, and she hoped she would have the chance to prove herself.

She climbed out of the bath, dried herself, and put on her pink dress. When she returned to her room, the twins had gone. Worried about being alone in the inn, she decided to search for another child or one of the Castle Seven. Going downstairs, she found the twins in the games room, playing Bar Pyramids. They asked her if she wanted to join in, but she said, 'No thanks. Do you know where the others are?'

'The boys are with Zoran and Robert in the bar,' said Hephzi, 'Alexandra, Lucinda and Sarah are about to go on an evening walk. I don't know where Anderson and Katharine are.'

'OK,' said Eleanor, and left them to their game.

She found the three women outside. 'Can I come on your walk with you?' she asked.

'I don't know,' said Sarah, 'we did say no children.'

Alexandra scowled at her. 'Oh, Sarah, don't be cruel. Of course you can come, Eleanor. But it won't be very exciting.'

'That's OK,' she said, 'I'm bored with the twins.'

Alexandra laughed. 'That's understandable.'

The three women had all changed their clothes, putting on lighter outfits for the evening. Although she was tired from the day's activity, Eleanor enjoyed the walk. It was a relief not to have to cover a certain amount of land in a specific time. The women all seemed in a light-hearted mood, and their conversation was flippant as they explored the surrounding area. Although Anderson had said this wasn't a community, there were a few houses here, and a large patch of land that had been cultivated into what looked like a small park. It was to here that the women headed, walking slowly. The heat of the day had been replaced by a mild breeze that made being outdoors much more pleasant. Eleanor thought she wouldn't mind living somewhere like this. It had the freedom of living outside a community without the fear of having no one to turn to if anything went wrong. She thought about how Alexandra had told her that she would be doing the same thing for the rest of her life – progressing from her current position to becoming one of the Castle Seven – and considered for a moment pursuing a different destiny, riding away from her community and establishing a life of her own somewhere else, where no one knew her, and where there were no expectations.

Occasionally, the three women would whisper to one another, which made Eleanor feel excluded, but she didn't complain because she was grateful that they had let her join them.

After one whispered exchange, Lucinda asked, 'What about you, Eleanor? What do you think of Anderson?'

'He gets grumpy with me for no reason.'

Lucinda laughed. 'He certainly does. But there's a reason for that, Eleanor. We expect more of you than we do of the others.'

'I know,' replied Eleanor, 'but why? Why was I chosen?'

Alexandra swooped down and gave her a hug. 'Oh, Eleanor, you have no idea of what goes on in our community, do you? We've been watching you since you were born.'

'But my parents . . .'

'We were never interested in your parents. They're nice enough people, and they raised you well, but your natural abilities have nothing to do with them.'

Eleanor didn't reply.

They continued walking, heading towards a large bandstand in the distance.

'Do you think they have music here?' Lucinda asked Alexandra.

'Maybe. It would make sense. People come here from miles around.'

As they drew closer, they saw a sign advertising a performance for eight o'clock that evening. Eleanor read the sign and asked Alexandra, 'What's a troubadour?'

'Don't you have your dictionary with you?'

'I left it back at the inn.'

She nodded. 'It's a singer, Eleanor. Do you want to stay and watch him?'

'Yes, please,' she said, 'if the rest of you do.'

'Why not?' said Lucinda. 'Shall we find a place to sit before everyone else starts to arrive?'

They found a spot on the side of a small hill that gave them a good vantage point. Eleanor felt extremely lucky to have gone with the women, and knew the twins would be jealous when she told them about this. A man came by selling jugs of lemonade, and Alexandra bought four, one for each of them.

'Well, this beats sitting in a bar, don't you think, Eleanor?'

'Definitely.'

The park was beginning to fill. There was a broad mix of people: families, old men and teenagers. Eleanor was self-conscious in her pink dress, as everyone else was wearing plain travelling clothes. But she felt safe with the three women, and although they had left their swords back at the inn, Eleanor was certain they would know what to do if they were in danger.

Eleanor's lemonade was so delicious that she sipped it as slowly as she could, sensing she wouldn't be allowed another.

The sky grew dark and the audience became increasingly rowdy, beginning slow hand-claps and throwing things onto the bandstand. Eleanor was surprised when the troubadour appeared and revealed himself to be a small, slight man, dwarfed by his large guitar. He smiled at the audience, but didn't introduce himself, instead immediately launching into his first song.

70

Eleanor had never had strong feelings about music before. It was something that was always in the background, but she rarely paid any attention to it. The minstrels in their community were sad, slightly crazy figures, little different to the beggars who ignored her because she was a child without money of her own. But this troubadour was different. It wasn't so much the music he played on his guitar, but the words of his songs, and the wonderful images they brought into her mind. Although all his songs were different, they fitted together into a larger vision that mesmerised Eleanor. He sang about the time before the fall of the kingdom, making it sound idyllic for some and terrible for others, and then about how the people had risen and overthrown this old order, which had been liberating, but had also left the world in disarray. Most of his songs returned to his own position, as a troubadour who had travelled the world seeking a place for himself, but being unable to find it, except in love. He couldn't have experienced the time before the fall of the kingdom himself, but he made it sound as if he had, and Eleanor loved hearing about it.

After a while, she sensed that the three women were not enjoying the music as much as she was. They had started arguing among themselves about the merits of the troubadour, and only Lucinda came to his defence. Eleanor could hear them whispering about her, and whether they should take her back to the inn. She kept quiet, praying she would be able to stay to the end of the troubadour's performance, and her prayer was answered because the women became quiet again and let her watch in peace. But as soon as the troubadour left the stage, they got up and started making their way through the crowd.

When they returned to the inn, Zoran was lying in the street outside, sleeping peacefully. Alexandra ran across and helped him up. He mumbled something but didn't complain as she led him back into the inn.

'Goodnight, Eleanor,' said Sarah, 'go and get some sleep. We still have another day of travelling ahead of us tomorrow.'

Eleanor nodded and went upstairs to her bedroom.

The twins were already asleep, so she tiptoed past them to the bathroom, cleaned her teeth, then got into bed. She spent at least half an hour eyeing the wooden man by her bed, convinced he was about to move. Whenever anything scary happened to Eleanor when she was about to go to sleep, she was torn between two impulses. One was to close her eyes and hope the frightening thing was a trick of her imagination; the other was to get up and investigate. But it was very hard to follow the second impulse, even if she knew that by doing this she would find that the scary figure standing by her bedroom door was really only a shadow thrown by a coat. Tonight she summoned up all her courage, sat up and went over to the man. As she peered at him, she became convinced that it wasn't her imagination.

Moments later, a large dark slit opened in the wooden man's side. It was a secret entrance into a system of passageways that ran throughout the inn. Michael had discovered this when he had examined the wooden man in his own bedroom, and he had followed the passageway to Eleanor's room. He jumped out and put his hand over her mouth, trying to stop her from screaming.

Although it took her a moment to work out what was going on, she managed to refrain from making any noise. Michael removed his hand from her mouth and pointed into the secret passageway. 'Come on,' he whispered.

He led Eleanor into the darkness, shutting the hinged door on the wooden man behind them. They were in complete blackness, and Eleanor worried about what might happen if they couldn't get out.

'Relax,' Michael told her, 'it's easy to open any of the wooden men from the inside.'

'Where are we going?'

'You want to see what the others are up to, don't you?'

'OK,' said Eleanor.

The first room they went to was Zoran's. The wooden man's eyes were secret peepholes and it was possible to see into the room without anyone knowing you were there. Eleanor felt guilty about spying on people, but curiosity overwhelmed her. Zoran was lying, out cold, on his bed, still wearing his clothes, with one boot on and the other off. He was snoring loudly.

'Come on,' said Michael again, and Eleanor followed him along the secret passageway to the next room. Through the peepholes she could see Sarah kneeling by her bed and saying a prayer.

Michael clearly wasn't interested in this, and he grabbed her hand, taking her further. This time he stopped by Anderson's room.

'Don't you want to see what they've been up to all evening?' he asked.

The way he said this worried Eleanor. She had a strong sense she was about to witness something she shouldn't, and when she looked through the peepholes she could see Katharine and Anderson studying a map, clearly planning the next day's journey. So Anderson had lied about how well he knew this territory. Eleanor couldn't believe it, and wished she could hear what they were talking about.

'Come on,' said Michael, 'let me have another look.'

'Wait,' Eleanor replied, but Michael pushed her away.

If Michael was going to be mean to her, Eleanor didn't want to stay here spying any longer, and she told him she wanted to go back to her bedroom. He was disappointed, but could see she was serious and took her back along the passageway, letting her open the door on her wooden man and go back to bed.

CHAPTER Nine

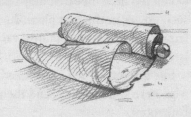

That night Eleanor dreamed of her family and friends back in the community. She had been feeling guilty since she told Anderson that Mary had a crush on him. Although it wasn't something they had raised with her, Eleanor felt under increasing pressure from the Castle Seven to forget about her family. At first she had been overawed by the sophistication of these adults, but recently her conviction that they weren't everything they imagined themselves to be had grown. She had always assumed that Robert, the quietest member of the group (usually because he was overwhelmed by Zoran's shenanigans), was a man of hidden strengths, but now she doubted this. He and the other men were young, so it was inevitable that they would misbehave on a mission like this, but surely someone a bit more mature could have been selected. After all, there was the whole community to choose from. And although the women could be kind, especially Alexandra, there was definitely some unresolved tension between them. Eleanor couldn't imagine how this motley crew would impress the important members of another castle, and wondered how on earth they had gained positions of such power in the first place. In comparison, her family seemed almost saintly, no matter how little they knew.

She got out of bed and looked across at the twins, who were still sleeping, and then went to the bathroom.

Anderson had arranged for them to have breakfast in a private room. He told them there were things they needed to go through after they had eaten, but before they began their final day of travelling.

Eleanor heard Lucinda tell him, 'I'm worried about the boy's leg. There's pus in the wound and he's still hobbling.'

Anderson shook his head. 'There's nothing to worry about. If you wash him and reapply the bandages after breakfast I'm sure he'll be able to survive until we get to the Greengrove Community. Once we reach there, we'll get a physician to examine him. But I really don't think it's serious.'

Lucinda nodded and backed away. Anderson looked across and gestured for the food to be served. Zoran was sitting opposite Eleanor, and he smiled, scratched his stubble and clutched his head.

'Crazy night, last night,' he said.

'Yes,' she replied.

'Breakfast,' he told her, 'just what I need. Where did you go last night? You weren't in the bar or games room.'

76

'No,' Alexandra answered for Eleanor, 'we went to the park.'

'There was a troubadour,' said Eleanor excitedly. 'He sang the most beautiful songs.'

'Music?' asked Zoran. 'Oh, I would've liked that. I'm sorry I missed that.'

'Well, if you didn't spend all your time getting drunk,' Katharine butted in, 'you'd realise there is life outside of a bar.'

'I didn't notice you at the park,' Alexandra said quietly.

'That's because I wasn't there, as well you know. I'm not interested in music. Besides, I was tired from all the travelling and needed an early night.'

Eleanor didn't comment on Katharine's lie, but Sarah said, 'You didn't miss much, anyway. It wasn't very exciting.'

After breakfast, Anderson handed out small sheets of parchment to everyone sitting around the table. Eleanor tried to read what she had been given, but the language was old fashioned and complex, mentioning duchesses, counts, court ladies and courtiers. It seemed to be an extract from a story, and although it was written in the style of a fairy-tale, the language seemed more serious. Eleanor frowned at the page. She recognised most of the words, but the content of the scene proved elusive, no matter how hard she tried to work it out. It was clear that the prose described some sort of elegant conversation, but it didn't seem like real people talking – definitely not the Castle Seven – and she had no idea what was going on. She gave up trying to follow it and waited for Anderson to explain.

'No matter how much instruction we give you, there are no hard and fast rules for how to conduct a successful conversation. I realise small talk probably seems incredibly boring to you, but pay attention to it. The easiest way to impress someone is to answer everything they ask in a light, funny, flattering way. And if you listen carefully enough to someone's small talk, it can give you a great insight into their character. Don't be afraid to be serious, but try to avoid being impertinent. Avoid gossip and' – here he stopped and stared directly at Eleanor, making her blush and feel everyone else was looking at her, too – 'don't try to buy favour by revealing another person's secrets. Never say anything to any member of the Greengrove Community that belittles any of the Castle Seven, and if they flatter you, watch out for an ulterior motive. If they patronise you, bear it lightly and never lose your temper. The sheets of parchment I have given you describe how a perfect conversation is conducted in courtly society. Study the words carefully if you get the chance today; use your dictionaries if there are any words you don't understand; and try to emulate that sort of interaction when you arrive this evening.'

With this, Anderson led them from the breakfast room. They went upstairs, gathered their belongings, and had an hour to themselves before they met outside the inn. Lucinda came downstairs with Stefan, his leg freshly bandaged. Eleanor could see she was worried about him, and hoped he would cope with the day's travelling. Climbing on to their horses, they set out again, for the final leg of the journey. Anderson set the pace, and they went fast, energised by their night's rest and the knowledge that their destination was close. Eleanor rode alongside the twins, whom she could tell were feeling a bit ignored by the rest of the group. She realised she hadn't made much of an effort with them, and in spite of their special, secret bond, it was likely they were beginning to feel lonely.

Hephzi clearly appreciated Eleanor's effort, and for the early part of the morning the three girls talked about their lives back at home. Eleanor was relieved to be away from the adults for a while, and pleased to have a conversation in a normal way, rather than trying to imitate the interaction of courtly society, whatever that meant. When no one was looking, she threw away her piece of parchment. She would be herself tonight, and hope that she was accepted. She already had a sense that the Greengrove Community would be far less stuffy than Anderson had made it out to be.

They rode until lunchtime, then stopped for another picnic, which had been prepared by the cook at the inn. Anderson walked round anxiously while everyone else ate, trying to hurry things along.

'Relax,' said Sarah, 'let us eat our food. A few more minutes won't make any difference. We'll be there in time.'

Anderson didn't pay attention to Sarah, continuing to pace behind them. Katharine got up and went over to him, whispering something in his ear and stroking his arm. Eleanor wondered why he was so worried.

After lunch, they mounted their horses for the afternoon's riding. The terrain wasn't difficult, and they continued at speed. Eleanor sensed something was wrong, but she didn't realise how serious it was until two hours later when Anderson abruptly brought his horse to a stop and leaped off.

'What's wrong?' Alexandra asked him.

'We've gone the wrong way,' he said. 'We're lost.'

'Are you sure?' she asked.

'I'm certain. It was just before lunch. I knew it then, but I hoped I was wrong.'

'It can't be as bad as you're saying.'

'Why don't you check your map?' asked Michael. 'Maybe there's a short cut that'll get us back on track.'

'I don't have a map,' Anderson shouted at the boy, letting him feel the full force of his frustration.

This struck Eleanor as strange, but maybe it hadn't been a map that he and Katharine had been consulting in his room the previous evening. She supposed it could have been the pieces of parchment he'd handed out.

'There is no map for this territory,' Alexandra told Michael in a gentler voice. 'You have to go by instinct.'

Hephzi started to cry. Alexandra went over to comfort her, shooting an irritated look at Anderson, who seemed shocked by the effect of his anger.

'OK,' said Robert, 'it's still only mid-afternoon. If you think you went wrong just before lunchtime, that's only two hours back. Then how far will it be from there?'

'About another four hours,' replied Anderson. He was beginning to sound calmer now.

Robert shook his head. 'There's no way we can keep going at full speed for that long. The children won't be able to handle it, especially the injured boy. But if you're worried about politeness, surely as long as some of us show up on time they'll understand about the rest.'

Anderson seemed to accept this. 'Yes, that might work. I could ride much faster if I didn't have to worry about the rest of you.'

'You should take one person with you,' said Robert.

'I'll go,' said Katharine.

'OK,' Robert replied, 'but you must give us precise instructions before you go.'

Anderson broke a branch off a nearby tree, then led the group to a patch of dry dust, where he used the branch to sketch out directions. Everyone watched intently, though Eleanor hoped someone else was taking it all in. Her worries were voiced by Alexandra, who asked, 'Are you sure this is a good idea? What if we get lost?'

'You won't,' said Anderson, 'if you stick to these directions. There are only two possible routes and we've already gone down the wrong one.'

This argument didn't sound especially convincing to Eleanor, but the others seemed to accept it.

Anderson and Katharine remounted, turned their horses round and rode off to the west, down a rough, muddy track that led to fields of bright yellow rapeseed stretching as far as they were able to see. For a long time, the remaining group stood silently watching, until Anderson and Katharine finally disappeared over the horizon.

Shortly after Anderson's departure, it started to rain. The group's spirits were already low, and the downpour didn't help. Everyone had waterproof coats and hats, but trekking through the rain slowed things down even more, and robbed the journey of any pleasure. Only the horses seemed to be refreshed by the falling water, especially Nathaniel, who started to pull ahead of the rest of the pack.

Michael moved his horse up alongside Eleanor's. 'What do you think all that was about?'

'The map business, you mean?'

'Yeah.'

'Well, we didn't see for definite that it was a map. It could have been anything.'

'Maybe, but why did he react so strongly when I made my suggestion?'

'You probably surprised him, that's all. He didn't know you were spying on him.'

Michael nodded. Eleanor felt guilty for reacting so crossly, but she still wasn't comfortable with what Michael had made her do the previous evening. She didn't like having secrets from the rest of the group, and disliked being pulled into duplicity with just one of them.

'How's Stefan holding up?' she asked him.

'He's OK. But it's clearly a lot more serious than everyone else is pretending.'

'Yeah,' said Eleanor, 'I wish they'd admit they're in trouble.'

'It's all part of their act, isn't it? We have to pretend everything's OK even when it isn't. I bet when they reach the castle they don't even mention Stefan's suffering until they've gone through all of their stupid rituals.'

Alexandra rode up behind them and Michael immediately blushed and went quiet.

'What are you two talking about?' she asked.

'Nothing,' said Eleanor. 'I just wanted to know if Stefan was all right.'

It took them longer than Anderson had estimated to reach the place where they should have stopped for lunch if they hadn't got lost. The rain fell heavily, and the sky was beginning to darken. Although the tension had eased when Anderson and Katharine had ridden off, there was a lingering sense of unease as everyone started to realise how much further they had to go.

Eleanor was riding alongside Alexandra when Sarah came up to her and asked, 'Do you think we should go back to the inn?'

'What? Why?'

'We've only got Anderson's word for how far away the Greengrove Community's castle is. What if he underestimated? He can travel a lot faster than us and probably didn't realise how long it takes the group to go anywhere. We don't want to show up at midnight. Or, even worse, get lost again. It's harder to travel when it's dark, we don't really know the way, and pitching a camp on this damp ground won't be much fun, either.'

Alexandra shook her head. 'I can see the logic in what you're saying, but we can't go back to the inn. Anderson would never forgive us if we didn't show up tonight.'

'Forget Anderson. We've got the whole group's well-being to worry about.'

'No,' said Alexandra, firmly, 'we continue the way we're going. We just have to pick up the pace, that's all.'

Six hours later, they reached the Greengrove Community's castle. Sarah had said they didn't want to arrive at midnight, but it was past one in the morning when they finally reached the castle's approach. The castle was very different to the one at the centre of Eleanor's community. It was on a hill, had a drawbridge and a portcullis, and looked much more forbidding. The tower had three semicircular bastions, with parapets at a lower level. It was obvious that at some point, probably many hours earlier, there had been plans to celebrate their arrival, but all the decorations had now been ruined by the heavy rain. The flaming torches had long since gone out and, instead of a welcoming party, there was a solitary guard, who was standing by the entrance keeping night watch and waiting for the bedraggled, depressed group to reach him.

'Hello,' he said, as they came close, 'my name is Jeremy. Everyone else is asleep, I'm afraid, but you'll be pleased that the party in your honour has been postponed until tomorrow.'

Alexandra asked, 'What about Anderson and Katharine?'

'Asleep. They were very tired when they arrived. But don't worry, the castle's cook has stayed up specially to make you a late supper. And I understand one of you requires medical attention.'

Robert stepped forward, holding the exhausted Stefan in his arms.

'Right,' said Jeremy, 'if the rest of you would like to head to the small dining room, on the other side of the court, I'll join you as soon as I can.'

Robert, Stefan and Jeremy walked towards a nearby staircase, while the rest of the weary party headed to the small dining room. It was connected to one of the castle's kitchens, and there was only enough space for one table. There was a chair for everyone in the group and they all sat down, relieved finally to have reached their destination.

'I can't believe Anderson and Katharine didn't wait for us,' said Lucinda, sounding genuinely annoyed.

'Yes,' Alexandra agreed, 'I have to say I'm surprised.'

'Maybe they thought it was impolite,' Sarah suggested. 'They probably thought if they stayed up and waited for us, their hosts wouldn't be able to go to bed themselves. And, anyway, it doesn't matter . . . I mean, what difference does it make?'

The cook appeared in the doorway. He smiled broadly and said, 'Ah, so you are here at last. I have made you a light supper, designed to restore your energy, but not to keep you awake. I hope you all like broth.'

The group, all of whom were so hungry and tired that they would have eaten anything, nodded and tried to sound enthusiastic.

'Good,' he said, 'I shall prepare this for you. In the meantime, I have put out bread and wine for you. And water.'

Everyone began to tear into their bread rolls. Eleanor's stomach felt empty and sore, and at first her mouth was too dry to chew the bread. She drank some water, which made her feel better. As tired as she was, she couldn't help feeling amused that after all their weeks of preparation for making a good first impression, in the end the only people there to greet them were a nightwatchman and a cook, both of whom didn't seem at all bothered about how they were addressed.

After their supper, Jeremy showed them to their sleeping chambers. Although she had never actually slept in her own community's castle, she couldn't believe its bedrooms were this luxurious. Ever since she was a very small girl, Eleanor had fantasised about sleeping in a four-poster bed. Now she had her chance. The bed took up much of the space, but there was still room for a full-length mirror and a dressing-table. She walked over and stood in front of the mirror, examining her reflection. Her blue dress had been ruined by the three days' riding, and was streaked with black mud. She wanted to throw it away, but thought it would probably still survive the ride back. Tomorrow she would wear something elegant, and behave in the manner that Anderson expected.

She undressed, put on her nightdress and climbed into bed. Even though she was completely exhausted, she still found it hard to sleep. It was almost as if she was too tired to sleep. Throughout the last part of their ride, she had been trying to conserve energy, worrying that when they reached the castle she would be required to engage in a conversation with someone before being allowed to go to bed. She was relieved this hadn't been the case, but now couldn't get rid of the energy. Nevertheless, it wasn't long before her head sank more heavily into the luxurious goosedown pillow and she drifted away from the frustrations of the day.

Chapter Ten

Eleanor awoke late the following morning, long after daybreak. She lay in bed for a little while, wondering anxiously about what might happen when she left her bedroom. She was surprised that no one had come to find her, and then started to worry that she was missing the celebrations. She pulled a white dress from her bag, and changed into it. She wished she had another pair of boots rather than the muddy ones she had been riding in, but there was no choice but to put them on again – she couldn't leave her bedroom without proper footwear.

As she stepped out onto the circular walkway, Eleanor noticed a slim figure with shaggy auburn hair slouching against the stone wall a short distance away from her. At the sound of her approach, the figure turned round. It was a boy, of about her own age, wearing an orange suit with a yellow cloak. He smiled at Eleanor and said, 'At last, you're awake.'

Nervously, Eleanor asked, 'Did I miss anything?'

He shook his head. 'Your friends are even lazier than you. They're all fast asleep. I'm Justin, by the way.'

He offered Eleanor his hand. She shook it, still feeling embarrassed. He was one of the first boys she'd ever seen whom she thought was attractive, and all of the Castle Seven's instructions on how to hold a polite conversation had vanished out of her head.

'And your name is . . .?' he prompted.

'Oh, I'm Eleanor. Pleased to meet you.'

'Likewise. Can I show you something, Eleanor?'

'Of course.'

'Follow me.'

Eleanor followed Justin as he led her round the circular walkway to the spiral staircase at the far end of it. She was scared as she looked down the great distance to the stone floor at least three storeys below.

'Scary, isn't it?' he said. 'Is your castle like this?'

She shook her head. 'Not at all. I mean, I haven't seen inside many of the private sleeping chambers of our castle, so I don't know how they compare, but the outside is very different, too. For a start, it's a completely different shape.'

Justin smiled. 'Yes, our rounded merlons are quite unusual.'

'But I think our castle is a lot bigger than yours. At least, as far as I can tell. I don't live in it, you see.'

'You don't live in your castle?'

She shook her head.

'Where do you live, then?'

'Oh, near by, in the community.'

Justin stopped and looked at Eleanor. It took only a second for her to realise she'd made a stupid mistake.

Katharine had told her they would be presented as a representative selection from their community, but she realised now that this had been a lie. The Castle Seven were trying to pass them off as children of noble birth. Eleanor tried to decide whether it was better to make excuses or tell Justin the truth. Uncertain which course of action Anderson would advise her to take, she decided on the latter.

'Oh, Justin, I'm sorry, forget I said that, please? I shouldn't have told you I didn't live in the Castle.'

Justin looked puzzled. 'OK. But why does it worry you?'

Even though she knew she was making a mistake, Eleanor couldn't stop herself blurting it out. And as she told Justin the story of the last few months, she watched his face to see how her revelations were being received, but he was impossible to read, making Eleanor regret her confession even more.

When she'd finished speaking, he said, 'Do you want to go up the staircase first?'

'It's OK,' she replied quietly, 'I'll follow you.'

Justin climbed to the top of the stair turret. Eleanor followed behind him, trying not to feel scared as they climbed higher and higher. When they reached the top of the turret, Eleanor felt a flash of vertigo.

'Are you OK?' asked Justin.

'I'm fine,' she replied. 'May I just keep still for a moment?'

'Oh, of course. Don't worry, we won't stay here for

long. I just wanted to show you where I watched you from.'

'Watched me?' she asked.

He grinned. 'You and your travelling companions. When you arrived last night.'

'You were still awake?' Eleanor asked, surprised.

'Oh, I can never sleep.'

'Me too,' admitted Eleanor. 'But why didn't you come down and say hello?'

'It may not seem that way, but I'm actually quite shy. I wanted to get to know one of you before I was introduced to your whole group. I did think about coming into your sleeping chamber.'

'Oh,' said Eleanor, 'I wouldn't have liked that.'

He nodded. 'That's what I thought. So I waited until you were awake. But I wanted you to know that I did stay up to see you arrive. And if there had been any problem, I would've helped.'

Eleanor had recovered from her vertigo, and was beginning to feel more brave. She took hold of Justin's arm, and edged towards the outer turret wall so she could take a look at the land below.

'How could you see us in the dark?' she asked Justin.

'I have very good night vision. It was part of my training.'

'So you had training, too. The Castle Seven told us that children of noble birth naturally had better skills than us.'

'Everyone needs some kind of training, Eleanor. You're not born knowing how to handle a sword. But I wasn't talking about the kind of education you're referring to. I was talking about military training.'

'Oh,' said Eleanor, embarrassed again, 'have you been in battles, then?'

'Not yet, thank God. But every castle needs to protect itself from invasion. You must know that.'

'Oh, no,' said Eleanor, 'we've never been invaded. That's why lots of people in our community don't believe we should have any communication with other castles. They didn't even want us to come here.'

'That's stupid,' replied Justin. 'Friendly relations with other communities are essential to maintaining civilised order.'

'That's what Anderson believes.'

'Is he one of the Castle Seven?'

'Yes. I'm sorry, Justin, can we go down now?'

Justin nodded, and they descended the spiral staircase. They headed past the level Eleanor had been sleeping on and continued down. At the bottom, Justin walked out and she followed him through to the main banqueting room. It was a large octagonal room with two wooden pillars on either side of a long table. Two wooden doors were shut at the bottom of a four-step staircase on the east side, and a small fire had already been lit in the large stone fireplace. Standing by the fire were Anderson, Katharine, Jeremy the nightwatchman and a fourth figure she didn't recognise.

'Dad,' said Justin.

The figure turned round. He was dressed in an

elegant black and ivory outfit, and looked like an older version of Justin, with a weary face and a black moustache.

'Oh, hello, Justin,' he said, 'I see you've located another of our guests.'

'Yes, Dad. This is Eleanor.'

Instead of introducing himself, Jeremy's father, whose name was Basker, turned back towards the fireplace and muttered to Anderson, 'At least one of your party has managed to drag herself out of bed before noon.'

Eleanor overheard this and said defensively, 'We had a very difficult day of travelling yesterday. Anderson went in the wrong direction and . . .'

Before she could finish her sentence, Anderson whirled round, his eyes aflame with anger. As he glared at her, she remembered what he'd told her only a few days earlier: *Never say anything to any member of the Greengrove Community that belittles any of the Castle Seven, and if they flatter you, watch out for an ulterior motive.* But she found she didn't care, and, shaking away the guilt, continued, 'It took us a long time, that's all. It's good for them to catch up on their sleep.'

Basker came across from the fireplace and said to her, 'It's not just a question of good manners, but also one of diligence. If we weren't a friendly community, I could dispatch an assassin to murder every last one of them while they slept in their beds.'

'But you *are* a friendly community,' Eleanor protested. 'That's why we've come here.'

Basker lowered his face until it was level with Eleanor's and asked, 'How do you know we're a friendly community?'

'Anderson told us.'

He turned and looked back at Anderson and Katharine. 'Ah, but my dear Eleanor, how well do you know your friend Anderson? He was responsible for guiding your group in the wrong direction and then he abandoned you in the wilderness. How do you know that wasn't all part of a deliberate plan? The three of us could have been plotting since the moment they arrived here.'

'Stop it, Dad, you're scaring her.'

'Am I?' he asked Eleanor. 'Am I scaring you?'

'No,' she replied truthfully. 'What you're saying is true. It is perfectly possible that we could have been led into an elaborate trap. But in order for this to happen, several betrayals of trust must have occurred: Anderson must have betrayed the rest of the Castle Seven, the Castle Seven must have betrayed me . . .'

'Not necessarily. Maybe Anderson is working alone, or with Katharine . . . Have you noticed the two of them spending a lot of time together recently?'

'Yes,' said Eleanor, 'they have. In fact, everything you've said makes perfect sense. But I know why you're saying all this to me. It's a test of faith. Without my faith that Anderson, Katharine and you are good people, it would seem as if I'm putting myself into a dangerous situation . . .'

94

'At least you're awake,' Basker said quickly. 'Do you see what I mean?'

'Of course. But the others have faith, too. They trust you to be friendly and generous hosts, to understand how difficult it was for us to get here from our own community.'

'Ah,' he said, 'touché. You are an extremely clever girl, aren't you? I fully expected you to say that you trusted the adults to make a decision for you. But no, you've followed your own intuition, and come to the correct conclusion. I am truly sorry, Eleanor, for doubting your faith.'

Eleanor flushed with happy pride, pleased she had managed to meet her first challenge. But she was still surprised that Basker had been so combative. She had expected small talk and polite conversation, not immediate threats that she was in danger.

Behind her, Zoran and Robert entered the banqueting room. They were followed by Alexandra, Sarah and Lucinda, and the rest of the children. Eleanor wondered if any of them had overheard her conversation with Basker, and if so, what they thought.

'Justin, can you go upstairs and fetch the others?'

'Where are they?'

'Oh, scattered all over the castle, I expect. You'll have to hunt for them.'

'OK,' he said, and went across to the staircase.

Basker's mood seemed to change completely now the rest of the group had arrived. He didn't say anything to them about the fact that they had stayed in bed so long, and Eleanor wondered why he had singled her out for an argument. Could he have guessed that she liked Justin, and, if so, was that what had made him angry?

'Come, come,' he said to everyone, 'sit. Jeremy, would you ask the cook to prepare brunch?'

Jeremy nodded and left the banqueting room. Eleanor sat down opposite Hephzi, who still had the red imprint of a pillow on her left cheek and a bad case of bed-head. Everyone looked dismayed to be awake, as if no amount of sleep could refresh them. Anderson whispered something to Katharine and then the two of them came across and joined Eleanor's table.

'Well done,' said Katharine to Eleanor, 'you handled that very well.'

'Apart from dropping me in it,' said Anderson.

'I know,' she said, 'I'm sorry about that. But I thought it was better to be honest.'

Anderson didn't comment, putting his chin on his knitted fingers and waiting for his food.

Slowly, other members of the Greengrove Community began to drift downstairs and take their seats on the other table. Justin and his father leaned in close together and whispered to each other. Eleanor watched them, sensing angry words were being exchanged. She wondered whether Justin was sticking up for her, and found this possibility oddly exciting.

Servants appeared and started placing bowls of scrambled eggs and wooden cups of orange juice in front of everyone who had come downstairs. Eleanor wondered if she should wait until everyone had come to the table, but as the Greengrove Community had made an immediate start on their food, she saw no reason to wait.

CHAPTER
ELEVEN

After breakfast, Basker told them that his community was extremely interested in their visitors. He had arranged for the group to be taken through the town – along with the Greengrove Community – on the back of large carts.

Zoran thought this sounded like a great idea. 'So,' he asked, 'what do we have to do? Wave at all the bystanders?'

'Yes,' said Basker, 'there will be some waving. But you'll also have to talk to a few of the people from the community. Some might even have gifts for you.'

'Gifts?' said Zoran. 'That sounds good.'

'Excellent. If it's all right with you, I think we should set off straight away.'

And so the Castle Seven and the five children headed out of the castle with the Greengrove Community and went down to the stables where four carts had been buckled to four pairs of imposing black horses. Zoran helped the children up onto their cart, and then the Castle Seven climbed onto their own transport. There were seats for everyone and

Eleanor found herself next to Stefan.

'How's your leg?' she asked him.

'Oh, it's almost completely healed since that physician looked at it. It was incredible, Eleanor, he dropped some sort of potion onto the bite marks and the wound just cleared up right in front of my eyes. It was so painful the night before last and now it doesn't hurt at all.'

'That's great.'

'How are you feeling, Eleanor?'

'I'm OK.' She hesitated, then revealed what was on her mind: 'Is this what you thought it would be like?'

'The mission? Or their castle?'

'Their castle.'

He shook his head. 'I think their community is very different to ours. I don't think most of the people here are allowed into the castle.'

'What makes you think that?'

'Well, if they were, why would they make us go through the whole community on a cart like this? It would be much easier for them to throw a big party like they did before we came away.'

'But I think they planned a party for last night. And then when we didn't arrive . . .'

'They could easily have postponed it until tonight. I think the party was always going to be only for the people who live in the castle. Anyway, I don't suppose it matters. I just get the feeling that these people think very highly of themselves.'

'So do the Castle Seven.'

He laughed. 'True.'

There was a driver at the front of the cart, and he cracked his whip on the horses' backs, urging them to set off. The cart was a bit unsteady, and Eleanor had to hold on to Stefan's arm to avoid being thrown off. Wheels splashed mud over the twins' dresses and they moaned loudly.

The expedition then went much as Basker had said it would. There were members of the community lining every street, and occasionally they would stop for a longer conversation with someone or to accept a small gift. Eleanor enjoyed the attention, although most people who approached them were more interested in the twins than her. Only when they reached their last stop at a small farm did anything amusing occur. A large farmer became so enamoured of Eleanor that he told Alexandra that he wanted to give the girl a present. Alexandra said this was fine, only for the farmer to wade into the middle of a dirty sty and grab hold of a huge pink pig. Wrestling the pig to the ground, he forced a collar around its hairy neck and brought it to the cart.

'Here,' he said, 'I want to give the girl my pig.'

'That's very kind,' said Alexandra, struggling to know how to respond, 'but that's far too generous.'

'No,' he said, 'I want her to have it.'

Alexandra looked helplessly across to Basker, who nodded and gestured for them to take it. Anderson got down from the cart, and went across to help the farmer load the pig onto the children's cart. The pig was nervous and made an attempt to run, but Eleanor quickly grabbed hold of its collar and yanked it back.

'See,' said the farmer, 'she already knows how to handle a pig.'

'It's a very nice present,' said Eleanor, 'thank you.'

Everyone else was trying to stifle giggles. Bidding farewell to the farmer, they turned their carts round and returned to the castle. When they got back, Basker took the pig from Eleanor and said, 'Don't worry, you don't have to look after the pig. We'll keep it with our livestock.'

Eleanor nodded, relieved, and handed over the leash.

CHAPTER TWELVE

Being friendly to so many people had exhausted Eleanor, and she was glad when the Greengrove Community asked the Castle Seven if they wanted some time to themselves. She was about to retire to her bedroom for a lie down when Justin came up to her and asked her to follow him. He took her back into the now empty banqueting room and led her over to where the four stone steps led down to two wooden doors. Then he took out a small key and unlocked the wooden doors, putting a finger to his lips and saying, 'You mustn't tell anyone I showed you this.'

'OK,' she said, and stood back as Justin opened the doors wide enough for them to slip through.

Behind the doors was another room, about half the size of the banqueting hall. This room was much darker, with five cannon, all pointing through gaps in the wall into the distance. Eleanor looked up at the ceiling and saw that this room was only three-eighths of the octagon that made up the castle. Although there were only five cannon, there were six gaps in the castle wall, and Justin led Eleanor across to the one that didn't have a cannon poking through it, telling her, 'Go on, through there.'

She stepped through the tiny square and found herself in a small private garden, separate from the rest of the castle grounds. The garden was so bright that it seemed to have the sun all to itself. She turned round and said to Justin, 'It's lovely.'

'No one knows I come out here,' he said. 'I think the only people who know this space exists are my mum, my dad and me.'

Eleanor looked back at the boy, touched by the faith he had placed in her.

He seemed embarrassed and struggled to find the right words before saying, 'I'm sorry about the way my father talked to you this morning . . . but it was worth it, in a way, because you really impressed him. He's always like that, though. He thinks you have to be tough at all times because otherwise someone will realise you're weak and take advantage of you. He doesn't understand that if everyone lived their lives that way, nothing would ever get done because of the constant questioning of other people's motives.'

As she listened to Justin trying to express himself, Eleanor realised his thoughts about his parents were much more complicated than her own. The way Justin felt about his family was more akin to how she felt about the Castle Seven. She couldn't imagine what it would be like to have a father like Justin's.

He gestured towards the grass, instructing Eleanor to sit down. She did so, and he came and sat down beside her. They didn't speak for a few minutes, as they both relaxed and enjoyed the sun.

Then Eleanor asked, 'Have you travelled much?'

He nodded. 'I do a lot of riding.'

'I don't mean that. Have you been to lots of other castles?'

'Six or seven. My father likes to move slowly. He believes in taking time to build up relations.'

'Like he's doing with us?'

'Yes, I suppose so. What about you, Eleanor? Have you visited lots of other castles?'

'No. This is my first trip.'

He smiled. 'Ah, so do you believe all the travellers' tales?'

'The only ones I've heard have been from Anderson or an innkeeper we talked to.'

'And what did they tell you?'

'Nothing exciting. Jokes, mostly. There were lots of things they were secretive about, or I didn't understand. But they were mainly just rude comments about people they'd encountered. Strange characters at various castles.'

'Strange characters?'

'Yeah.'

'So you haven't heard the really weird stories, then?'

'I don't think so. What sort of thing are you talking about?'

'Well, as so little is known about the time before the fall of the kingdom, even by official historians and storytellers, there are two versions of how the different communities came about. Most people believe that the country hasn't changed too much, and that the communities are grouped mainly in a geographical way.'

Eleanor looked at Justin. She didn't understand exactly what he was saying, but she felt that didn't matter, and sensed he was leading up to something significant.

'Put it this way, I know that my ancestors have always been in charge of this castle, but I don't know what position they used to occupy in the kingdom . . .' He tailed off, staring earnestly at Eleanor, but clearly sensing he was losing her.

She wanted to look as if she was taking everything he said seriously, but these were evidently questions he had puzzled over for years. It was hard for her to follow them when, until recently, she had known nothing of the world outside her own community. She touched his hand. 'I'm sorry, Justin, can you explain what you mean?'

He nodded. 'It's like this. We're a long, long way from the central castle, as far as I'm aware, if, that is, such a thing even exists any more . . .'

Eleanor thought about this for a moment, and then said, 'OK, I'm with you so far.'

'Right. My parents are very careful about what they allow me to read . . .'

'I thought your dad wanted you to know about everything . . .'

'Oh,' he said, 'that's all bluster. He has Jeremy guard that library night and day, and although I've sneakily managed to find out more than they want me to, all that I can come up with is that our main role must have been to provide a second line of defence from invaders . . . I think that's why we have those cannon.'

'Invaders from where?' asked Eleanor. 'If all the castles in the kingdom were united back then . . .'

'Other kingdoms.'

'Other kingdoms?' repeated Eleanor, flabbergasted. This possibility had never occurred to her. Just thinking about the concept made her head hurt.

Justin noticed her bewilderment and said with a smile, 'But, anyway, I'm distracting myself. What I meant to say was that the other legend that explains how the various communities formed themselves is that after the fall of the kingdom similar sorts of people grouped together.'

'That's what the Castle Seven believe,' Eleanor told Justin, pleased to be able to offer something to the conversation.

'Is it?' he said excitedly. 'Do they have any evidence?'

'I don't think so.'

'Well,' he considered, calming down, 'if that's true, then it might explain why more people don't visit the castles further afield: it's because they're terrified about what they might find there.'

'What are you suggesting? That the people might be evil?'

'I don't know. There are all kinds of outlandish stories. I think it's a lot of silly superstitious nonsense, but who knows, there might be some truth to it. Why do *you* think people don't travel more extensively?'

Eleanor shook her head. 'I'm not the right person to ask about this, Justin. I've never travelled outside my own community before, and I barely even realised such a thing was possible. Your family might have been careful about what kind of books they let you read, but my education's been even more controlled. Until I joined the Castle Seven's group of children, my teachers didn't even want me to know there were other communities.'

He nodded. 'That's not unusual, Eleanor. I imagine most of the people from all thirty-nine communities are brought up in the same way, apart from those who choose to live in the wilderness or roam, but even the bravest people seem scared about travelling beyond the limits they set themselves. What's out there, Eleanor? What's out there that's so terrifying?'

'I don't know,' replied Eleanor. 'Maybe your father's right. Maybe the biggest threat comes from people you can't trust.'

Justin abruptly sat up. 'We should go back now, before anyone finds us.'

'OK,' she said, and followed him through the hole in the wall.

CHAPTER
THITREEN

Eleanor went back to her sleeping chamber and lay on her bed. While she was waiting for the private time to be over and someone to come and fetch her, she drifted into a nap. She felt even more tired today than she had done when they were travelling. She supposed it was all the past exertion catching up with her, and the sense that – in spite of Basker's attempts to frighten her – she could afford to relax. She snoozed until she heard a knock on the door, and then sprang up, in case it was Basker. Eleanor didn't want him to know she'd been sleeping again.

She got out of bed and went to the door. It was the twins, who told her she was required to come down for an afternoon of music and conversation with some of Justin's cousins and friends. They were to go out into the garden while the adults talked inside. Eleanor felt uneasy about not hearing their conversation, but was unable to resist the twin's enthusiasm. In any case, she knew the adults wouldn't want her to eavesdrop.

As she followed the twins, Eleanor thought about how there had been no real discussion about how long they might be staying at the Greengrove Community's castle. Now her blue dress had been ruined by riding, she had only six outfits to choose from, and was worried about what she would wear if they stayed longer than a fortnight. She had a sense that they would be here only a few days, but maybe she'd got the wrong impression. There was one thing she was certain about: the Castle Seven's story about why they were going on this expedition had to be only part of the reason. It didn't make sense for them to have come all this way just to maintain friendly relations. There was definitely some form of negotiation going on, and she had a sense that something serious would be decided during the afternoon's debate.

The twins led Eleanor through the castle and into a different garden from the one she had been lounging in with Justin. There was already a large group waiting there, including several faces she didn't recognise.

For the first time, Eleanor found herself using the social skills she had been taught over all those arduous weeks of training with the Castle Seven. Only she wasn't using them in order to further conversation, but instead to find a polite way of avoiding it. Everyone was friendly and kind, and they all seemed to welcome the chance to talk. Eleanor, however, had only one interest, which was to remain alongside Justin. She could tell their earlier conversation was still on his mind, and she wanted him to know she was thinking about it, too. She had never thought about the thirty-nine castles before, not with any real curiosity, but now she yearned to visit them all. Would that be possible? She was still young, and had already decided that the destiny offered to her wasn't something she really wanted to pursue. Although she felt far too shy to mention it to him, Eleanor now thought a perfect future might be to become a traveller with Justin, as long as they would be welcome wherever they went. Her castle no longer felt like the one home she would have in her life, and she was even less comfortable here. Justin, too, would no doubt one day want to leave his family and this castle. It was clear that if this didn't happen soon, it would become a prison to him.

Justin seemed pleased she had come to join him, but, apart from acknowledging her presence, he said little. Eleanor didn't mind. If Justin didn't want to talk, she wouldn't either.

The minstrels who took up position in the garden with their simple wooden instruments were similar to the ones who played at Eleanor's castle, and were certainly nowhere near as good as the troubadour she had watched in the park with Lucinda, Sarah and Alexandra. Eleanor realised the reason why the music didn't touch her soul in the way the troubadour's had was because there were no lyrics. During their dancing lessons, Sarah had told Eleanor that the very finest music had no words, but she assumed she must be talking about a different sort of music to any she had heard. Certainly she found the insipid tunes of the minstrels far less compelling than the stories the troubadour had spun in song.

Eleanor had assumed she would spend the whole afternoon standing next to Justin in silence, so it took her completely by surprise when he turned to her and said, 'Would you like to dance?'

No one else was dancing, but Eleanor couldn't resist this opportunity to make her dream come true. The details were different, as they were in a garden rather than a banqueting hall, but that had been true of everything else she had imagined ahead of time. The others laughed and clapped, and within a few minutes several other pairs had started to twirl around the garden. Eleanor noticed Hephzi dancing with Michael and wondered if she had revealed how she felt about him. The minstrels seemed pleased that their silly music was being appreciated, and started to play with more enthusiasm. They extended the tune long past its natural end, as if worried the dancing would finish when the music did.

Only once Justin had stopped twirling her and they were standing together did Eleanor start to worry. Maybe, as this part of her vision had come true, her other, more frightening imaginings would also come to pass. She feared that, if this did happen, it would be her own fault, because she had accepted Justin's invitation. But even these worries couldn't quash the giddy happiness that swelled inside her.

×

They were left in the garden for hours. Although the minstrels gamely attempted to keep playing, by the time it started to get dark Justin took pity on them and told them to pack away their instruments.

'But we were told to keep you entertained until the adults finished their meeting,' the tallest one protested.

'It's OK,' said Justin, 'I doubt they expected you to play for this long. They've probably lost track of the time. Besides, I think we've heard every tune in your repertoire. Two or three times, if I'm not mistaken.'

'That's true,' admitted the minstrel ruefully. 'But I must ask you, would you tell your father that you told us to go?'

'Of course. Don't worry, I'll make sure you're paid.'

The minstrel blushed and, nodding, backed away. Justin started walking towards the castle.

'Where are you going?' asked Eleanor.

'I'm going to find my father. It's disgraceful that he's kept us waiting for so long.'

He strode away from her. She waited a moment, and then, unable to stop herself, followed. He didn't seem to mind, and the two of them entered the castle together.

Eleanor was amazed by what she saw. At least five people were talking at once, with Basker banging his fist on the table and bellowing over everyone else. Anderson and Katharine were huddled in a corner, watching the conversation with eager interest. The children had clearly interrupted an enormously heated debate.

So Eleanor had been right. There was something at stake. As soon as the adults noticed them, they fell silent. Apart from Basker, who immediately demanded, 'Yes?'

Eleanor could see Justin was afraid, but he held his head up high as he said in a calm voice, 'We've had enough. You've been keeping us waiting for hours now.'

'Oh, Justin, what's wrong with you? You have the minstrels for entertainment, don't you?'

'I sent them home.'

'What? Why?'

'They were exhausted. Do you realise how long you've been talking in here?'

'Oh, I'm sure it hasn't been that long. What's the time?'

'Seven,' Sarah told him.

'Oh,' he said, 'well, I'm sorry, Justin, but we haven't concluded our discussions.'

'Can't you postpone them until tomorrow?'

'It is getting late,' said Alexandra. 'Maybe things will resolve themselves when we've had a chance to sleep on them. Besides, we're all tired, and we're not getting anywhere.'

'No,' said Basker, bringing his fist down on the table again, 'we will never reach this point again. Hours of vital negotiation will be lost, and neither side will remember its position. As it is, this interruption might already prove fatal.'

'Oh, relax,' Alexandra replied, 'we can all remember what's been said. Besides, I'm hungry . . .'

'Me too,' said Zoran, 'let's break for dinner.'

Eleanor watched Basker. He seemed to be weighing up options, presumably trying to decide what would happen if he really lost his temper. She sensed that if the adults weren't here watching he would be furious with Justin, and felt that as soon as he got his son alone he would punish him. But at the same time, whatever they were discussing was clearly quite sensitive, and he seemed to decide he couldn't risk an outburst of unchecked emotion.

The group rose from the tables. Some of the Greengrove Community looked exhausted, but most of the Castle Seven remained relaxed. Eleanor wondered whether they had been winning the discussion, and if this was the reason why Basker had seemed so reluctant to concede even a temporary conclusion.

'Shall we go through to the banqueting room?' asked Justin's mother. She looked pleased that her son had interrupted the discussion, and as the group walked away from the table, she came across to him.

Eleanor chose this moment to approach Anderson, hoping that if she spoke to him now he might reveal more than he would after he'd relaxed.

'So,' she asked, 'what have you been talking about?'

'Nothing you'd be interested in, Eleanor. We're just making plans for the future.'

'What sort of plans?'

He turned away. 'We hope to have a long-lasting relationship with the Greengrove Community. This will involve things to do with other castles, other communities. Nothing that need concern you.'

Eleanor realised she wasn't going to get anything more out of Anderson, and asked him if she should go and fetch the others from outside.

'Yes, Eleanor,' he said, 'why don't you do that?'

The rest of the evening was quiet. Basker told them that the promised celebration of their arrival had been postponed until the following night, and after dinner there was little to do. Everyone retired earlier than usual, drained from the travelling or the day of discussion. Eleanor found it much easier to sleep than she had the previous evening, and dropped off within a few minutes. That night she dreamed of Anderson and Katharine. They were somewhere in the Castle, having a conversation she couldn't hear because she was hiding behind a pillar. Katharine was angry at Anderson, and he was protesting she'd misunderstood something he'd done. Even in her sleep, Eleanor was puzzled by the dream, and by the time morning came she was no closer to understanding its meaning.

CHAPTER
FOURTEEN

Once again Justin was standing outside Eleanor's sleeping chamber, waiting for her. He had a black eye.

'Did your father do that?' she asked him.

He nodded. 'We were arguing and then we started fighting and he ended up giving me this. But I gave as good as I got.'

Eleanor looked at the proud boy standing in front of her and felt a swell of sympathy for him. She knew her friend Mary back in her community didn't get on with her parents, but at least they never physically fought with her. If this was what a noble family was like, she was glad she came from a normal background. Her parents might have failed to nurture her, but at least they were kind. She regretted their lack of ambition, but that had to be better than the strange madness that gripped Basker and made him want to best everyone in any situation, even his own son.

Justin turned and walked away. Eleanor followed him, and the two of them went down for breakfast. On the way they ran into the twins.

Hephzi smiled at them both and said, 'The beds here are amazing, aren't they?'

Eleanor nodded. 'I had a great night's sleep.'

Hephzi took a long look at Justin, and Eleanor knew she had noticed the black eye. But she didn't mention it, asking him instead, 'Do you know what we're going to be doing today?'

'I don't think we'll be doing anything. Probably be listening to those stupid minstrels again.'

'Oh,' she said, 'please no. Can't we go exploring or something?'

Justin considered this. 'Actually, that might be a possibility. Let me talk to my mother.'

'I don't know why they even brought us along,' Beth protested. 'I mean, those children yesterday, apart from your cousins, Justin, they don't live here, do they?'

'No,' admitted Justin, 'this is a family castle.'

'I knew it,' she said. 'This is so stupid.'

'Do you wish you hadn't come here?' Eleanor asked her.

'She's feeling homesick,' Hephzi answered for her sister. 'We both are.'

Beth shook her head. 'It's not just that. I thought this was going to be an adventure.'

Eleanor felt the same way, but she didn't want to admit this in front of Justin. She knew he hated his father, but he had to live here after they had gone and it seemed cruel to insult his home and family.

'I'll speak to my mother,' Justin repeated.

✕

The Castle Seven, apart from Katharine and Anderson, were in low spirits. Zoran in particular didn't seem to be looking forward to another day of discussion, and sat in a sad slump as he ate his breakfast. Eleanor wished again that someone would tell her the truth about what was going on so at least she could feel they were being bored for a good reason.

After breakfast, Justin came over to Eleanor and the twins and told them, 'It's fixed. My mother says I can take you out to the lake. It's one of my favourite places to visit.'

'Will we be allowed to swim?' asked Hephzi excitedly. 'We went past a lake on the way here, but we were only able to paddle.'

'Yes,' he said, 'and we have trunks and swimming costumes for everyone.'

This lifted the mood. There was an obvious relief at not having to suffer another afternoon with the minstrels, and everyone was also pleased to be getting away from the castle.

'What about me?' asked Stefan. 'I can't get my bandages wet.'

'Let me just unravel them and take a look,' Eleanor told him. 'After all, you said the wound had almost healed.'

Stefan flinched, but didn't back away as Eleanor bent down and unwrapped the bandages. As she did so, she saw there was no sign of the wolf's bite marks and Stefan's skin was pink and healthy.

'See,' she said, 'you're fine.'

Justin was the only child from the Greengrove Community who went out that afternoon. Eleanor was pleased to have him in their group, as it meant that they now naturally fell into three pairs. That was the way they rode, too, with Eleanor and Justin up front, the twins behind them and Michael and Stefan at the back. Justin didn't like to talk much as he rode, but Eleanor was happy simply to be alongside him and to be reunited with Nathaniel. The atmosphere was more relaxed without the adults, and there was a definite sense that everyone wanted an afternoon of fun. Eleanor mentioned to Justin that maybe the adults would get along better if they allowed themselves time to socialise.

He replied, 'It's my father. He won't let anyone relax until he's got exactly what he wants. That's why he keeps postponing the party.'

'What I don't understand is why the Castle Seven made such a big deal about the importance of social interaction . . . If Anderson had already met your father, he must've known what he was like.'

'Dad can be deceptive. That social stuff is only to lure in people. It's how he gets them to discuss things with him, but then, when the proper talk starts, he becomes really hard.'

'But what's it all about?'

'Building castles in the air.'

Eleanor looked at him, astonished. 'What?'

He laughed. 'It's an expression. I don't mean it literally. My father is an extremely arrogant man. You remember what I said about how people don't know what most of the other castles are like?'

She nodded.

'Well, my father doesn't believe any of the travellers' tales. He thinks the other castles are full of scared people who don't go exploring because of all these silly stories about what they might find. He thinks the time before the fall of the kingdom was a golden era, and believes people are crying out for a new leader. But in order to become that person he needs to prove himself.'

'How does that involve the Castle Seven?'

'I don't know. He won't tell me. Maybe he's prepared to share leadership. That's probably what they've been doing for the last two days, dividing the thirty-nine castles between them.'

They didn't talk about this for the rest of the day, preferring instead to swim and play. But none of them could relax completely, as they were all aware that something serious was happening back at the castle. By late afternoon they were exhausted, and ready for the ride home.

Expecting to find the adults still deep in discussion, they were surprised to discover instead that the meeting had been concluded and they were waiting for them to return so they could begin the party. Everyone went upstairs to change, and when they returned they had a small evening meal before the banqueting room was transformed for the celebration. The minstrels reappeared, looking sheepish and choosing their most inoffensive songs in an effort not to annoy anybody. A small group of guests joined the Castle Seven and Justin's family, and everyone talked and drank.

Eleanor approached Anderson and asked, 'So the meeting went well, then?'

He nodded. 'There was a completely different atmosphere this afternoon. Everything progressed much more smoothly.'

The adults did seem happier. Eleanor was relieved the tension had disappeared, but was still uneasy about being at the castle. She didn't accept any of the excuses Justin made for his father, and couldn't feel comfortable with the hospitality of such an unkind man.

After a few hours of conversation, Basker announced it was time to play a game. One of the minstrels produced a blindfold and Justin wrapped it around Eleanor's head.

'OK,' said Basker, 'Eleanor, go into the corner and count to two hundred and fifty. Justin will guide you.'

Eleanor felt Justin place his hand on her back and gently steer her over to the corner. She started counting.

Justin whispered into her ear, 'Go slower.'

She did as she was told, reciting the numbers at a relaxed speed. When she reached her target, Justin nudged her gently from behind and she started walking.

'Steer me, steer me,' she told him.

'It's OK,' he said, 'I'm here. Just keep walking and I'll direct you.'

'What am I supposed to be doing?'

'Finding the others. It's hide and seek.'

'Oh,' she said, 'I thought so, I just wasn't sure.'

'My dad's being stupid again. It'd be almost impossible to find everyone without my help, but don't worry, relax, I'll direct you. If I push you straight, go forward. Left, go left. Right . . . well, you get it.'

'OK.'

Eleanor continued walking. To begin with she felt extremely disorientated. Even putting one foot in front of the other was difficult, and, although she trusted Justin, the prospect of walking round the castle blindfolded petrified her. Justin directed her out of the banqueting room and up the spiral staircase. Her fingers stroked the stone as she went. Justin kept climbing behind her until, she realised, they were about to go out onto the south wall walkway. Clutching the wall, she told Justin she didn't want to play any more.

'It's OK, Eleanor, it's just a game. I'll protect you.'

'But it's dangerous.'

'No, it's not. The walls are too high for you to stumble over them. You'd be perfectly safe even if I wasn't here. Besides, I think you'll find this is the best place to start.'

Taking a deep breath, Eleanor stepped out. She could hear giggling in the distance and started to walk towards the sound. Every time Justin poked a finger into her back she went in the direction he instructed, and within a few steps she felt her hands collide into the wood of one of the minstrels' instruments.

'OK, OK,' she heard him say, 'you got me.'

'Shall I go back downstairs now?' Eleanor asked Justin.

'No, I think you might want to stay out here a little longer.'

Eleanor took his advice and continued down the narrow walkway. As she found herself clutching Basker's cloak, she heard him say, 'Oh, hello, Eleanor, yes, well done, you've caught me. And, look, who else is this here? Two for the price of one.'

Another giggle revealed that she had also located Justin's mother. The way these two adults were so happy to give themselves up worried Eleanor, but maybe they were simply tired of playing the game. Her parents were like that sometimes. Justin held her and asked her to wait while the adults passed by, and then he directed her right around the walkway until they reached a different spiral staircase on the other side. She was going to let the adults go first when she heard Basker say, 'No, no, Eleanor should go down before us.'

Justin took a moment to reply. Eleanor sensed something strange was going on, but started walking down the stairs anyway. Justin was no longer behind her and she was suddenly very scared. With every step she nearly stumbled. Her hands frantically gripped the stone wall to keep herself upright. At least, until she reached the bottom step, when she fell through a giant hole in the floor.

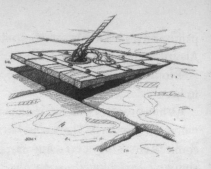

Chapter Fifteen

As she fell, Eleanor grasped for the walls, but her fingers found no purchase. She was terrified that her legs would break when she hit the ground, but instead she landed on Anderson's shoulders and the blindfold fell off.

The rest of the children, and all of the Castle Seven, were already locked in the oubliette. If Eleanor had had her dictionary on her, she could have discovered that an oubliette is a secret dungeon with access only through a trapdoor. Although she had heard all about the dungeon in her own castle, she had never seen it. It hadn't occurred to her that there would be a dungeon in the Greengrove Community's castle, and she was astonished that it had this high, narrow shape.

The group had been led into their prison only a few minutes earlier, at the start of the game, but already panic had started to set in, and they had climbed up onto one another's shoulders, trying to get high enough to bang on the square of padlocked wood that imprisoned them. Eleanor immediately realised their effort was futile, and, unable to help herself, started to panic. This set off Stefan, Michael and the twins, and Alexandra was forced to shout at them to calm down.

'Stop it,' she said, 'I'm sure they don't mean to keep us here for ever.'

'Why have they done it, then?' snapped Lucinda.

'Isn't it obvious? They're going to invade our community. They'll go there pretending to have news about us, and then storm the Castle.'

Eleanor thought about her family and Mary. The idea that they might be attacked upset her even more, but she breathed deeply, trying to hold in the tears.

'This is your fault,' Sarah told Anderson. 'If you had been more generous in our discussions, he wouldn't have resorted to this.'

Anderson didn't reply.

Slowly, pressing against the wall, the people in the human tower moved downwards. There wasn't enough room for everyone to stand upright, but they tried to reposition themselves into more comfortable positions. Eleanor remained at the top of the cramped bodies.

'Let's look on the bright side,' said Zoran. 'They could've killed us.'

The twins started crying again.

'Thanks for that, Zoran,' replied Alexandra crossly. 'I think we have to accept we're trapped. But they might not be organised enough to attack our castle. They could be trying to scare us.'

'Well, in that case, it's worked,' said Lucinda. 'How long are they going to leave us here?'

As the group squabbled about their predicament, Eleanor tuned out. She was as scared as the others, but, like Zoran, she took comfort from the fact that they were still alive. Basker was crazy and violent: if he was going to kill them, he would have done it already. And surely he couldn't keep them imprisoned for ever. Then again, he must know that there would be a fight when he released them. So what was his plan?

Eleanor also found it hard to believe that Justin had betrayed her. The game of hide and seek had been so carefully arranged to distract her from what was going on that he must have been part of it. But why had she been the last person to be put into the oubliette? And if he were abandoning her for good, surely he would have offered her a final message – a whispered 'goodbye' or 'I'm sorry' – before she fell through the hole in the floor. The fact that he hadn't said anything left her with two possibilities: either he'd been lying to Eleanor from the moment they met, or he might be coming back to rescue her. But then another alternative struck her, one that made much more sense. Perhaps Justin had known this was his father's plan from the beginning, and during the last couple of days had been trying to dissuade him from going through with it. That explained the whispered exchanges, the arguments, Justin's black eye. If that was the case, what would Justin do next?

It was a while before the group stopped talking, as if they believed that as long as they were coming up with possibilities and suggestions there was still hope. But eventually depression set in when they realised no one was coming for them and there was nothing more they could do tonight except try to sleep. Getting such a large group into comfortable lying positions was almost impossible, and the only way they could do it was to curl up together, hold on tight, and try not to wriggle too much. The adults went at the bottom, with Zoran, Robert and Anderson bearing the rest of the group's weight. It was easier for the children than the adults, being small enough to lie straight. Eleanor closed her eyes, acknowledging in her heart for the first time that they really had no way of knowing how serious this situation might be. It seemed perfectly possible that they could all die here, cramped inside this tiny space. Death wasn't something Eleanor had contemplated properly before, although she knew it could occur every time she became involved in a sword-fight. The Castle Seven had never revealed that she might face this kind of danger, though, and that it might happen in this undignified way. The worry that this could be her last night on earth didn't stop Eleanor from sleeping, however, and she didn't suffer from insomnia, as she desperately accepted sleep in the hope that dreams might bring a solution to her predicament.

Chapter Sixteen

They were awoken the following morning by a bucket of cold water being thrown down from above. Eleanor immediately sat up, finding herself in more pain than she'd ever been before. Her body ached so badly that, even though it annoyed the people beneath her, she instantly rolled backwards and forwards to rid herself of cramp. Everyone else seemed to be in similarly intense pain, and for a moment the only sounds were the group's moans and groans.

Eleanor looked in the direction from which the water had come. Jeremy, the nightwatchman, grinned down at them. 'Good night, everyone?'

No one replied.

'I take it you'll all be wanting breakfast.'

The group remained silent, as if wary this might be a joke. Jeremy went away for a minute and then came back with a large basket of food.

'I'm going to pass this down to you. Now, make sure you all behave.'

Jeremy passed the basket down to Anderson, who started giving out food to the other members of the group. It hadn't been long since their last meal, but fear that they might not be fed at all had made everyone ravenous. Jeremy handed down a jug of water and then closed the hatch.

'See,' said Alexandra, 'they're feeding us, so this has to be a temporary thing. I think the invasion possibility makes the most sense.'

The group finished the food and moved round the small space, everyone rubbing their arms and legs. They seemed to have passed through hysteria into a sense of dull resignation. Still, it was obvious that they couldn't survive down here for ever.

When Jeremy returned, Alexandra asked him in a very serious voice, 'Surely you could let the children back up? They're not going to cause any harm.'

'Oh, come on,' Jeremy said with a laugh, 'do you think we don't know that you've trained them to fight?'

Alexandra was shocked that the nightwatchman knew this, and looked round, as if trying to work out who had given away this information. Eleanor realised it had been her, in a conversation with Justin. So was it true, then? Was he genuinely not to be trusted?

Jeremy closed the hatch on them again.

Unsurprisingly, the day passed extremely slowly. The adults took it in turns to tell stories. Eleanor found Zoran's the most amusing, but the rest of the adults had to keep stopping him when he went too far. Sarah told stories about her family history, and Eleanor enjoyed these, too, especially those that reminded her of the songs the troubadour had sung that night in the park. Lucinda also provided at least an hour's entertainment with her recollections of life working in an inn and the pompous behaviour of some of the travellers that had passed through. The Castle Seven encouraged the children to tell stories of their own, but they felt too scared to make up anything.

Michael was especially agitated, and when the group fell silent, he hit his fist into his hand and exclaimed, 'There has to be a solution, there has to . . .'

But if there was, at present no one had any idea what it might be. It was impossible to tell what time it was from inside the oubliette, but after Jeremy had returned with an evening meal, it seemed inevitable that they would be spending another night in this terrible situation.

After they had eaten, no one said anything. It was impossible for them to continue light-hearted conversation, and if they talked seriously it would make everyone even more desperate. The members of the group slowly began to prepare themselves for another night in the cell. Then the wooden hatch opened again.

'Eleanor,' hissed Justin.

She looked up.

'Quick, everyone,' he said, 'push her up.'

The group climbed up onto one another's shoulders, and pushed Eleanor so she could catch hold of Justin's hand. He stepped back, braced himself and yanked her up.

She looked at him in happy amazement. 'So you weren't in on it?'

He looked sad. 'This was the only way I could help you, Eleanor. I needed to wait until my father had gone before getting you out.'

'So what's happening? Is your father invading our community?'

He nodded. 'You're the only hope. If I help you escape, you have to ride without sleep for as long as possible. That's your only chance to get back before them and raise the alarm. They were meant to leave this morning, but there was a problem with the horses and they couldn't set off until this afternoon. They're five hours ahead of you, but they don't know the way, and they'll be going slowly. They'll be sleeping at night, but for as long as possible you'll have to do without rest.'

She clutched his arm. 'Aren't you coming with me?'

'I can't,' he said. 'My father knows how to get to me. All my weak spots. It's much better if you go alone. I've prepared your horse for you.'

Eleanor nodded, scared, but too excited to protest. She understood the wisdom of what Justin was saying, and was galvanised by the fear of what might happen to her family and friends when the Greengrove Community attacked. There were people in her community who could fight: strong physical types who would be able to stand up to Justin's family.

As if reading her mind, Justin said, 'They have an army, but it's not a big one. They're relying on the element of surprise, and they're going to pretend that they come in peace. The only chance of this situation being avoided is if your castle is prepared for the attack and you imprison them before they realise they've been rumbled.'

'I'm not sure if our dungeon is big enough for an army.'

'They won't have to imprison the whole army. They'll need to be physically restrained, but once your community has captured my father, they won't risk continuing the invasion.'

Eleanor considered this. 'OK, I understand. But what's going to happen here? Won't Jeremy be angry when he sees I've gone?'

'I've taken over his duties, at least as far as the oubliette is concerned. He's a lazy man, and won't investigate unless it's absolutely necessary. But the rest of the Castle Seven and the children will have to stay in there.'

'Justin, I'm not sure they can cope.'

'It'll be different now. I'll explain what's going on and at least they'll have hope. And I'll make sure that at some point I help each of them out of the oubliette and let them stand or walk for a while, as long as they remain out of sight.'

'But what happens when your father doesn't return?'

'I don't know yet. Let me work that out. You have enough to worry about.'

Eleanor nodded. Justin led her through the castle to the banqueting room, unlocked the wooden door, and then told her to go through one of the cannon-holes. She did so, and Justin showed her how to get to the edge of the grounds. Justin hadn't prepared Nathaniel but a white horse, just like the one Eleanor had ridden in her dreams. She took this as a good omen and climbed onto her new horse. Leaning in close, she whispered to him, 'We've got a long way to go together, you and I. You must be strong, and support me all the way. You have to go fast, lives are at stake.'

The horse whinnied, which Eleanor accepted as a sign that he understood, and they rode off together.

CHAPTER
SEVENTEEN

As soon as she started riding, Eleanor realised that it was not as easy to find the right route as she had imagined. She thought she remembered the way they had come exactly, but now everywhere looked unfamiliar, and she knew that the most important decisions were the ones she made right at the beginning. When Anderson and Katharine had taken a wrong turning, it had been near the start of that particular leg of the journey. There were only two or three obvious routes, but she knew that to stand any chance of getting back to her community in time to save the Castle she couldn't afford to retrace any steps.

She looked for a landmark: a tree she recognised, anything to convince her this was the right place to start. Finally, she looked for the ground that seemed most freshly trodden. Finding a big stretch of overturned earth marked by hoof prints, she decided this was her path.

It was dark now, and soon she was in almost complete blackness. She realised that if she *had* taken the wrong route, there would be no way of telling until morning. But all she could do was ride on, and pray she was right. Another worry was that she might run into the Greengrove Community. She had no way of knowing if they would be stopping at the inn that her party had stayed in on the last night of their journey, or whether they would be camping for the night.

Eleanor realised that she had to stop her fear if she was to get through this. If she kept thinking about all the terrible things that might happen, she would go mad and never complete her mission. It occurred to her that in all their weeks of training, the Castle Seven had failed to equip her for any of the actual problems she had faced. They hadn't spent any time on how to survive if you were separated from the group, or how to conquer fear. It was up to her to work out these things alone.

She thought back to how she had felt when she faced down the wolf. Before that encounter, all of her phobia had come from thinking about what *might* happen if she met a wolf. But when it *did* happen, she found she could deal with it. There were lots of terrible things that *might* happen if Basker and the Greengrove Community arrived at her castle before she did, but they hadn't happened yet. And, as long as she remained calm and continued on her mission, there was a strong possibility that they would not happen. She had to focus on this. But in order to do so, she had to control her imagination and stop it conjuring up horrible images. As she rode, awful visual flashes popped unbidden into her mind with almost every hoofbeat, accompanied by the memory of the dreadful music the minstrels had played on their wooden instruments.

Eleanor realised that the best way to settle her mind would be to try to control the music she was hearing. Thinking of the night she had gone to watch the troubadour, she started imagining how he might compose a song about her adventures. She pictured the small, slight man with his large guitar up on the bandstand and wondered how his song might begin. He would probably start with her leaving the Castle on this first mission; then the second verse would be about her encounter with the wolf. He'd smile, pause and slow the tempo, moving into a romantic ballad about her and Justin for the next two verses, before returning to his original tune to sing about what she was doing now. Eleanor tried to construct a tune from the many she half remembered, and before long the trick had worked and the images in her mind became more positive.

Having relaxed her thoughts, Eleanor put her head down and rode. She kept going like this for several hours. There was no sign of the Greengrove Community, which worried her. If they were riding without sleep, too, it would be impossible to overtake them.

Soon it grew lighter and Eleanor realised it wouldn't be long before dawn. She didn't feel particularly tired, but thought it would be best to try for at least a few hours' sleep. She had a long way to go and needed to keep up her energy. Worried about being discovered, she led her horse away from the main track and looked for somewhere to sleep in the woods. Taking blankets from the horse's back, she made herself a small bed. Then she lay down and went to sleep.

She slept for three hours, but as she didn't have a watch she thought it had been much longer and awoke in a panic. Jumping on her horse's back, she rode off at a gallop. At first fear kept her alert, but after she had been riding for a while tiredness took over and she continued in a strange daze, somewhere between the real world and her sleeping one.

When she heard splashing and saw one of the Greengrove Community's army washing himself in a stream, it took a moment before Eleanor realised she wasn't dreaming and that she was in real danger of being discovered. Yanking back her horse, she desperately leaped from her saddle and tried to find a safe place to hide in the bushes. The soldier looked up, and went to the bank for his sword. Eleanor's heart pounded as the soldier looked in all directions, unable to decide where the sound had come from. So they *had* set up camp for the night. Fortunately, at that moment another soldier came down to the stream and the man washing himself decided this was what he had heard.

Eleanor wondered what to do. At this moment, she had two choices. One was to move away from the main track until she was safely past the camp, and then keep ahead of the Greengrove Community. The other was to stay behind the army for the time being, and choose a safer time to get past later. After a minute's thought, Eleanor decided on the second course of action.

Scared, she moved to a place where she could safely monitor the camp without being seen. They seemed to be getting ready to move. Eleanor couldn't see Basker, but the army seemed relaxed. This made her even angrier than she would have been if she'd caught them preparing for battle. The idea that they were so convinced of their victory that they weren't even scared about fighting infuriated her. She was still frightened, but now she felt more certain than ever that she could help her community beat their opponents. Justin had told her the Greengrove Community was going to pretend they'd come in peace, and she could use that to her advantage. She was sure the army would not leave without a battle, though.

Eleanor waited until the Greengrove Community had moved on and then started riding a short distance behind them. They went slowly, and she had to keep stopping to avoid being seen. They passed the inn where she and the Castle Seven had stayed on their last night of travelling, but they didn't stop, and Eleanor realised they were going to camp again for a second night. She decided that this would be her chance to get in front of them. It was a risky strategy, and she would have to be very careful about how long she slept, which was difficult because she didn't have an alarm.

The Greengrove Community rode all day, and Eleanor remained near by, following their trail. When they finally stopped to set up camp, Eleanor crouched in the darkness and waited. As she hid, she suddenly heard the sound of heavy breathing, and, terrified, whirled around.

Her heart nearly stopped when she saw it was a wolf. Although she had no way of telling, Eleanor was convinced it was the same animal that had attacked Stefan. Trying to make her voice sound light, she addressed the animal: 'Oh, it's you again. Well, perhaps you can help me. Up ahead are some very bad people. If you want to bite someone, that's where you need to go.' The wolf stared at Eleanor. She braced herself, expecting it to lunge at her again, but instead it ignored her and headed off in the opposite direction.

Eleanor stayed where she was, waiting for the army to go to sleep. When she was certain it was safe, she led her horse away from the main track and rode round the camp. Aware that this was where she could get her greatest lead on the Greengrove Community, she rode solidly until just before dawn, when, once again, she allowed herself a few hours' sleep.

CHAPTER EIGHTEEN

After her sleep, Eleanor rode as fast as she could, knowing that if she kept up a decent speed, she would be able to reach her community by nightfall. There was always the possibility that the Greengrove Community might stay at the inn where Lucinda had once worked, but Eleanor didn't think this was likely. She had decided that the reason why the Greengrove Community was camping throughout their journey was to avoid any advance word of their plans reaching Eleanor's castle, and it was unlikely that they would abandon their strategy at this late stage.

Eleanor rode past the inn and continued at speed. Her mind continued to race, her brain determined to complete this mission before her body could.

She reached her community at dusk, and rather than head straight for the Castle and the skeleton staff keeping order there, she stopped outside her parents' house. Leaping off the white horse, she ran through the front door.

April looked up. 'Eleanor! What's wrong?'

'Where's Dad?'

Jonathan came through from the bedroom. 'I'm here. What is it?'

'The Castle Seven have been kidnapped! Dad, you have to come with me.'

'Of course. Where?'

'The Castle. We have to tell them what's happened.' April looked at her husband.

He gestured for her to stay where she was. 'Don't worry,' he told her, 'I'll sort this out.'

Eleanor and her dad left the house and started running towards the Castle.

'There's more to this, isn't there, Eleanor? Something you couldn't tell Mum.'

She nodded. 'An army's on the way. This is our only chance to prevent an invasion.'

They went through the arched stone doorway and Eleanor ran up to a tall red-haired woman standing alone in the bailey. Eleanor launched into an explanation, but was talking too fast for the woman to understand. She told her to calm down and try again. Eleanor did so. When the woman understood what had happened, she immediately started to panic.

Jonathan touched her arm. 'It's OK,' he told her, 'we still have time. Now, how do we get the army together?'

CHAPTER NINETEEN

Eleanor and Jonathan had four hours' sleep that night. Then, before dawn, they rode out with the skeleton staff and the community's army. They knew the only way to avoid a full-scale invasion was to reach Basker while the camp was sleeping, but also realised that he would have left someone keeping guard.

Jonathan had been appointed the unofficial leader of the group. Eleanor was assisting him, and when they pulled the army off the track he asked her, 'Do you know what Basker's tent looks like?'

Eleanor shook her head.

'It's OK,' he replied. 'It doesn't matter. There's only one option. We have to find the lookout and make him take us to Basker.'

'What if he sees us first and raises the alarm?'

'Then we've failed. Eleanor . . . I don't want to ask you to do this, but you're the one who's most likely to get up close to him without being seen. Did the Castle Seven teach you how to handle a sword?'

She nodded.

'Then take mine. Remember, you aren't going to use it. Just threaten him. Quietly. I'll be close by behind you. As soon as you've persuaded him to take you to Basker, put your arm in the air and I'll come over.'

Eleanor swallowed. She couldn't believe her father trusted her with something so dangerous. As scared as she felt, she was determined to prove to him that she deserved his confidence. Jonathan told her the route he wanted her to take, and she followed it. First she went over to the row of trees by a nearby ditch, then, after slowly making her way, one by one, behind them, she dropped into the thick, wet grass and crawled across to where the camp started. As she did so, she saw a soldier leaning on the handle of his sword. His head was lowered and he appeared to be sleeping. Eleanor looked around for a second guard, unable to believe that her task could be this easy. Then she crawled over to the sleeping man and went round behind him, putting her sword across his neck. She couldn't believe what she was doing. There was no way she could bring herself to harm this man, but even threatening him was terrifying.

She patted the guard on the back and he jerked awake.

'What?' he said, then quickly fell silent when he noticed the sword.

'Take me to Basker.'

'Don't kill me.'

Eleanor raised her arm. Her father ran across and took the handle of his sword, letting his daughter step back. The soldier then showed them to Basker's tent. Jonathan opened the flap and leaned inside, putting his foot on Basker's chest.

Basker looked up, recognised Eleanor, and laughed. 'Is my son with you?'

She shook her head.

'He sent you alone? I can't believe I raised such a cowardly boy. But you . . . you're not a coward, are you? It must have been difficult to get past us unseen.'

Pride forced Eleanor to hold up her head and say, 'It was easy.'

'Basker,' said Jonathan, 'let me make this easy for you. Our army is as strong as yours, and prepared for battle. If you wish, I could give the signal and we can have a bloodbath. Or you can tell your army to turn back.'

Basker laughed again. 'Then what happens to me?'

'I think the trade is obvious. We will dispatch people to ride to your castle and pick up the Castle Seven. When they've returned safely, you'll be free to go.'

Eleanor watched Basker. She was surprised how calmly this transaction was being discussed and expected him to respond in a burst of violence. But, although he happily fought with his son, he seemed to prefer discussion with adults. After a moment's thought, he said, in an even voice, 'What if I don't believe you?'

'We are a peaceful community,' replied Jonathan. 'We have no interest in war. If you're looking for a castle to overthrow, there are plenty of others to choose from.' He removed his foot from Basker's chest.

Basker rubbed his chin and considered this. 'I suppose I have no choice. OK, I accept your offer.'

Eleanor was amazed. She expected Basker to pull some last trick, but instead he simply got up, woke his army, and told them they had to turn back. He also told them to grant safe passage to whoever came to free the Castle Seven, and went peacefully to be held hostage with the skeleton staff. She supposed he did this because he was a pragmatic man and could sense that this time there was no way of winning. He might not like defeat, but he realised he was at the mercy of this community and if he tried to fight he would be killed. Far better to let this one go and wait for the opportunity for revenge.

CHAPTER
TWENTY

There was a lot of frantic discussion when they got back to the community. Eleanor's mother was not at all happy about her exhausted daughter returning to the Greengrove Community's castle. But as Eleanor was the only one who knew the quickest route, where the Castle Seven were being kept and who to trust, she had to go. In order to appease April, it was agreed that Eleanor would be accompanied by her father, and, although they would travel fast, there would be no more nights without sleep.

During the day's travel, Eleanor told her father stories about her previous trips and what had happened on her journey. He looked worried whenever she mentioned anything frightening that had happened and cross whenever she talked about the Castle Seven. Eventually, she was moved to tell him, 'It wasn't their fault what happened, Dad. And this adventure's done a lot of things for me. It's opened my eyes, and completely changed my life.'

'They also put you in mortal danger, Eleanor. I can never forgive them for that.'

146

'They didn't know what was going to happen. They thought the Greengrove Community were friendly.'

Jonathan didn't say anything in response, but from the expression on his face Eleanor could tell her father didn't trust the Castle Seven. What he said was true – they had put her in danger – but, given that things had worked out safely, she didn't think it was worth being angry with them. She knew that part of what made him cross was that she had trusted these people and they had let her down.

They had to camp out that night, but it passed without incident. Eleanor felt much safer having her father with her. It had crossed her mind that someone from the Greengrove Community's army might try to attack her in her sleep, but this didn't happen, and the following morning she awoke feeling more relaxed than she had in days. The end of her mission was in sight, and she hoped that nothing terrible would happen when they reached the castle.

CHAPTER
TWENTY-ONE

Justin was waiting for them. 'Eleanor,' he said when she rode up to him, 'you did it.'

She smiled and dismounted, with Justin holding her horse's reins. 'Justin, this is my father, Jonathan. Dad, this is Justin.'

Justin shook hands politely, and then looked at the ground.

'How is everyone?' Eleanor asked.

'OK,' he said, 'I looked after them really well for the first few days. But when Jeremy found out what had happened to my father he insisted on taking over care of the prisoners. He still can't quite accept that you managed to capture Dad and thinks it's some kind of trick.'

'He's not going to give us any trouble, is he?' Jonathan asked.

'No,' said Justin, 'I don't think so. He wouldn't want to risk you doing anything to my dad in retaliation.'

'OK,' Jonathan replied, 'but let's not give him the chance to think up another plan. We should move quickly.'

Justin nodded. 'Let's go.'

They tied up their horses and went to the oubliette. Jeremy was standing guard, his long face unhappy. Justin made him move back as he raised the wooden trapdoor. As he did so, Eleanor could see Anderson at the top of the people inside. Justin stretched down, took hold of Anderson's arm, and hauled him up. Anderson thanked Justin and walked over to where the armour was stacked. Jonathan helped Anderson on with his breastplate and handed him his sword.

Katharine was the next person to be helped out. She shook her black hair and went over to Jonathan, who handed over her sword.

Suddenly, Anderson drew his sword and said, 'Thank you. Now, I'm afraid you four need to get into the oubliette.'

'What?' Justin demanded.

Anderson laughed. 'You don't think your father would have gone to the Castle without a back-up plan, do you?'

Jeremy was delighted. 'I knew it!' he cheered.

'Well, Jeremy, I'm glad to have come through for you. But Basker should have told you more. You treated us horribly while we were in the oubliette, and for that you're going to have to suffer, too. Now, get in.'

Katharine seemed delighted by Anderson's words. She had been smiling at him all this time, and couldn't stop herself from going over to give him a kiss. In this moment, Jonathan grabbed three swords. He threw two towards Eleanor and Justin and pointed his own at Anderson, shouting, 'I will never forgive you for endangering my daughter's life.'

Eleanor picked up her sword. Two days before she had held a sword to a soldier's throat, but this felt different. She couldn't imagine stabbing Katharine or Anderson, and knew that if she did, it would change her life for ever. She thought back to everything Anderson had taught her, and the strange feeling she'd had ever since she'd been shown how to sword-fight: that one day she would have to put the knowledge and skills she'd learned into practice. Now, it seemed, the moment had come.

But, before Eleanor could do anything, Anderson laughed again and said, 'We're not going to fight you. You're not stupid. You know that harm's going to come to someone, and it's most likely to be Eleanor.'

Jonathan's face was going red. 'How dare you threaten my child?'

Anderson ignored him. 'Besides, what threat do we pose to you now? We're not interested in our community any more, and if you've imprisoned Basker, then our whole mission has been a failure. It would be easy for us to return with you, but the charade is over. And you're going to let us go.'

No one moved.

As soon as he realised his words had worked, Anderson grabbed Katharine and the two of them ran from the Greengrove Community's castle.

'Should we go after them?' Eleanor asked her father.

He shook his head. 'No,' he gasped, 'Anderson's right. It's too dangerous.'

'So what are we going to do?'

Jonathan looked around. 'Is everyone ready?'

There was general agreement.

'Then let's go.'

CHAPTER
TWENTY-TWO

Eleanor had assumed it would be easy to persuade Justin to leave his castle and come back with them. She had seen what her father had done to him after a trivial argument, and couldn't imagine what he might do after a betrayal of this magnitude. She even feared for the boy's life. But Justin said that his mother would protect him, and that he thought his father might even be proud that he'd finally stood up to him.

'Are you sure?' Eleanor pleaded.

'Yes. He's a politician, not a psychopath. And he still hopes that one day I'll follow in his footsteps. I can't abandon my family, Eleanor.'

'But what about your plans to travel? To see the rest of the thirty-nine castles?'

'That will happen one day. If I leave now, my father will be my enemy for ever. And it will turn your community into a target. But as long as I'm here, keeping an eye on him, I'll have some control. And when he dies, I'll undo any damage he's done.'

Eleanor smiled. 'You're very brave, Justin.'

He kissed her. 'And so are you.'

As Justin broke away, Eleanor tried to remain calm, not wanting Justin to see her cry. There would be plenty of time to miss him later. For the moment, she just wanted to memorise the face of the first boy she'd ever kissed.

As they began the long trip home, Eleanor thought that Hephzi must have told Michael about her feelings for him, because the two of them were riding alongside each other hand-in-hand. Beth and Stefan remained alone, looking miserable as they trekked with the others at the back.

Alexandra, Sarah and Lucinda had tried to thank Jonathan and apologise for what had happened, but they soon realised what he thought of them and now kept out of his way. Only Zoran and Robert seemed unaffected by their adventure, as if this was exactly what they'd expected to happen.

Chapter Twenty-three

HAIL THE CASTLE SEVEN

A few days after they had returned safely, Eleanor's mother decided to throw a party for her husband and daughter. When the five remaining members of the Castle Seven heard about this plan, they persuaded her to hold it in the Castle's grounds. April was reluctant to accept this offer, but over the last week she had become friends with the parents of the rest of the children, and they persuaded her that it would be a good way to honour her family.

The party was an enormous celebration, probably the biggest the community had ever seen. Word of Jonathan's and Eleanor's bravery had spread among the people, and even those who had refused to come to the first leaving party for the Castle Seven were happy to attend this time. The failure of the Castle Seven in their first mission had amused many people in the community and made the Castle seem much less intimidating.

The Castle was decorated even more elaborately than it had been for the first party, and there was an equally generous supply of food and drink. Although

Eleanor had once felt estranged from her family, tonight she loved her parents more than she ever had before, and felt proud of everything her father had done.

Early in the evening, Eleanor had the chance to talk to Michael and tell him how happy she was that things were going well between him and Hephzi.

'What about you?' he asked. 'You liked the boy at that castle, didn't you?'

She nodded. 'But he had his own life to deal with. I just hope his father's not too horrible to him.'

'He'll be all right,' Michael told her, 'he seemed strong.'

At midnight, Sarah and Alexandra came up to Eleanor and Jonathan. Alexandra said, 'I'm sorry to intrude, but could you two come with us.'

Jonathan, who had had a couple of drinks, said, 'Listen, this is my party. Can you please leave us alone?'

'I know you're angry with us. And for good reason,' Alexandra said in a polite voice. 'But we need to discuss something with you.'

Their gentle entreaties eventually persuaded Jonathan to leave his friends and go with the two women into one of the side rooms. When he and Eleanor entered the small space, he saw that the other three remaining members of the Castle Seven were already waiting there.

'Not you lot again,' he said. 'What do you want this time?'

'We have a request,' said Alexandra.

'Eleanor's not going on any more of your stupid missions.'

'We don't need just Eleanor,' Alexandra told him. 'We also need you.'

'Me?' he asked.

'Yes. You came through when we failed. We want you to join the Castle Seven. Well, Six, I suppose.'

Jonathan considered this. Eleanor watched him, knowing there was no way her father would refuse such an honour, no matter what he thought of the people bestowing it.

'You're not going to put her in danger again.'

Alexandra shook her head. 'Our next mission will be much safer. We've been in contact with several other communities in nearby areas. They're worried about Anderson, Katharine and Basker teaming up and coming to attack them. All we have to do is visit them and agree a mutual pledge to defend one another from any form of invasion and continue friendly relations. The threat of five armies should be enough to deter those three from attacking anyone.'

'So we're just going to be visiting other castles?'

'Exactly.'

'And how do you know there aren't any more Baskers out there?'

'We've met these leaders, and we trust them.'

'You trusted Basker.'

'Not completely. It was Anderson and Katharine who drove us into that alliance. And we know now that they did that for reasons of their own.'

'Well,' said Jonathan, 'I'll have to talk to my wife.'

Eleanor and Jonathan walked out onto the battlements for a quick conversation before returning to the party.

'Mum's not going to be happy,' Eleanor told her father.

'You let me talk to her,' he replied. 'If we choose the right time, it might be all right. She's certainly enjoying the attention tonight.'

'Yeah,' said Eleanor.

'Am I going to have to do all those lessons that you did?' he asked her. 'Learn how to eat properly and dance, and things like that?'

'I don't know, Dad. It's not that hard.'

'Well,' he said, 'I hope this is a good idea.'

'It is. Don't worry.'

Back in the party, Eleanor wasn't sure how she felt. Her father had come through and rescued her this time, but she wasn't sure she wanted to go on missions with him all the time. She was proud of him, and loved him, but this had been her thing. Then she felt selfish. She had seen so many exciting things on her first mission, and she'd wanted someone to share them with. Her father might not always understand, but, then again, she wouldn't always be with him. Alexandra, Sarah, Lucinda and the twins would also be there.

Something important had happened to the Castle Seven and the children. They had all learned something from their first mission: that it didn't matter what skills you had if you trusted the wrong people.

Eleanor saw her friend Mary standing alone. She couldn't believe she hadn't noticed her until this moment, and quickly ran across.

Mary embraced her. 'I was so scared,' she said. 'I couldn't believe what happened.'

'Me neither. And Anderson . . .'

'I can't believe I liked him,' said Mary. 'Besides, I didn't really, it was just a silly crush.'

'I knew that.' Eleanor smiled. 'But I have a confession to tell you. I'm afraid I told him how you felt about him.'

Mary blushed. 'I can't believe you did that. What if he comes back to get me?'

'He won't,' said Eleanor. 'He told me off for betraying your confidence.'

'What if that's what made him turn evil?'

'Oh, I doubt that,' said Eleanor with a laugh, 'I doubt that very much.'

Eleanor and her family stayed late at the Castle that night. They were almost the last to leave, walking home as the dawn broke. Although Eleanor and her father had decided not to tell April about their secret meeting just yet, she was curious, and knew something was up.

'So,' she said, 'are you two going to tell me what's making you so cheerful?'

Eleanor traded a look with her father.

'Oh,' replied Jonathan, 'I'm grateful for the party, that's all. It's wonderful having such a kind wife.'

'OK,' she said, not buying this, 'if you don't want to tell me yet, that's fine. But I'm going to find out what happened. Trust me on this.'

Jonathan smiled. 'I trust you, April.'

When they reached their house, Eleanor went straight to bed. As she was drifting off to sleep, she could still hear her parents talking. Her mother was asking Jonathan if the Castle Seven had given him money, and he was laughing and saying no. Eleanor didn't like keeping a secret from her mother, but she knew it wouldn't be for long, and she trusted her father to choose the right moment to tell the truth.

She was just relieved to be back in her own bed, too exhausted to worry any longer, and completely unaware of the danger that lay ahead.

ACKNOWLEDGEMENTS

Many thanks to Suzy Jenvey, Philippa Milnes-Smith and Helen Mulligan, for making this happen.